IN THE STREETS OF VINEGAR HILL

IN THE STREETS OF VINEGAR HILL

A Novel

William A. James Sr.

iUniverse, Inc.
New York Lincoln Shanghai

IN THE STREETS OF VINEGAR HILL

iUniverse books may be ordered through booksellers or by contacting:

iUniverse
2021 Pine Lake Road, Suite 100
Lincoln, NE 68512
www.iuniverse.com
1-800-Authors (1-800-288-4677)

ISBN-13: 978-0-595-42550-1 (pbk)
ISBN-13: 978-0-595-68015-1 (cloth)
ISBN-13: 978-0-595-86879-7 (ebk)
ISBN-10: 0-595-42550-X (pbk)
ISBN-10: 0-595-68015-1 (cloth)
ISBN-10: 0-595-86879-7 (ebk)

Printed in the United States of America

Dedicated

to

Sarah, Deloris, Barbara,

William, Jr.

Constance, Hakim & Acacia

Introduction

Gabe, who lived just over the hill from Abe Jones, (See: *Living Under The Weight of the Rainbow, 2005*), left his modest home in rural Fluvanna County, Virginia at the age of sixteen. His mind was filled with memories of the horrible life he had been forced to endure. His family was one of the poorest Black families in Fluvanna, that lived in one of the poorest neighborhoods in that area.

To make matters worse, Gabe believed his father's cruelty to him was directly related to the unending cycle of poverty that surrounded them. The question constantly on Gabe's mind was, *Why does dad always take his spite out on me?* After sixteen years of his dad's meanest to him and his mother, Gabe decided that, *I'll just quit school, leave this madness all behind, and jump into life just like that.*

He'd seen Abe Jones go off to Charlottesville, and although he'd not heard from his buddy since he left a couple weeks ago, he thought that Abe must be doing all right. He hadn't returned home, anyway.

So Gabe figured, *That's it. I'll go up to Charlottesville just like Abe did and get started up yonder. How bad could it be?*

Once Gabe arrived in Charlottesville, at the bus station in fact, he became acquainted with three characters who forced their "friendship" on him. They were Bobcat Hinter, and his tough guy sidekicks, Bubbles Quayles and James Killeen. These hooligans became Gabe's unwanted protectors, and so-called, "walk-partners." Gabe was present with them when Bobcat "yoked" (or robbed), a University of Virginia student, who died as a result of the beating he had sustained from Bobcat.

Gabe lived in fear of being identified as one of the "boys" involved in the murder of the UVA student. Somehow his name never came up as he watched his hoodlum "friends" get killed one at a time. He worried that he might be next. He had informed on Bobcat and his pals. He feared that one of them might find out and avenge himself by killing him. He couldn't imagine going back home, and didn't know where else to go, so he stayed put, and was full of fright and paranoia.

The fear of Detective Clemm Doll, a terrible "white-racist," scared Gabe even more. He believed that Doll was responsible for killing James and Bubbles. He worried that Bobcat and he might be next. Then Gabe heard the news.

Vinegar Hill, a very old Black community, was going to be razed to the ground. The day came for the whole area to be demolished, and Gabe watched as Vinegar Hill was crumbled to the ground. He grieved inwardly and outwardly while the wrecking cranes, steam shovels, and bulldozers destroyed a part of Black Charlottesville's *Communal Soul*. He felt as though the history of these people was being torn asunder. He was witnessing the murder of a way of life, a people's identity, the soul of Vinegar Hill, for no good reason. Gabe's anger inspired him to write down what he had seen and experienced, so that we would never forget what had happened to him and to *Us!*

PART I

▼

CHAPTER 1

▼

Gabe Owens peered out the windows of the green and white passenger bus at passing vehicles as the bus pulled into the Trailways terminal in Charlottesville, Virginia. The bus hit a speed bump that threw Gabe forward. He grabbed the overhead rack to steady himself. Luggage and carrying cases were stacked up to the ceiling. Gabe wondered, *Where are all these people going with all this luggage and stuff?*

His nose had taken all of the cigarette smoke he could stand on the way up to Charlottesville. The sour bodies, and faint mix of alcohol that climbed on the bus with some didn't help either. Gabe just wanted some fresh air.

On the way up to the city, he'd been annoyed to the hilt, too, at the constant bickering by some very outspoken people in the back of the bus. Then, the bus came to a final stop, the doors swung open wide, and the brakes "swooshed!" when the air was released from them.

People immediately crowded into the aisles toting handbags, small suitcases, briefcases, and ladies' handbags. All of the Black passengers in the back of the bus stood up. A rotund man wearing a two-piece gray business suit, a red tie over a white shirt, squeezed by Gabe and almost stepped on Gabe's feet with his shiny brown shoes. Gabe surmised, *This man got to be some professional guy, just judging from his clean-cut appearance. He didn't have to push me aside with his huge butt, though!*

"Excuse me son, got to get to the toilet, fast," the dressed-to-the-nines guy allowed. He hustled up to where the white passengers' line began. Then he stopped!

Another old looking guy, Gabe hadn't seen get on the bus at any of the stops on the way up to Charlottesville, speaking in a screaky voice allowed, "Son, aren't you going to get off now? I thought I heard you tell the bus driver when you got on that you were coming up here to Charlottesville. Well you're here."

Feeling a strange sensation as the old guy spoke to him, Gabe turned to take a good look at the old-timer. He was bent just a little, wearing a plaid shirt, faded red with what was left of a pair of Levi Jeans. The thought popped into Gabe's mind, *There's something weird about this one! This guy's eyes are burning right through me. His voice is hoarse and deep, like it's coming from deep-down in his guts. I can feel every word he's saying inside of me or something.*

The old-timer narrowed his big, brown eyes, wiggled his wide, nut-brown, nose, bunched his heavy gray eyebrows almost together and got ready to utter something further to Gabe.

"Some call me *William Griot.* In the near future, when you're filled with questions about this place up here, just ask around after me. You'll get to know the meaning of my name and what it stands for. I could tell you a lot right now, but you'd not be the wiser for it. Get wisdom, son. Get understanding," came out of the old guy's ashy lips in sort of a low-wail.

Down within Gabe a hot sensation ignited. Gabe wondered, *Who is this guy?*

"Son, I can see within you. You're running away from a lot of pain—yes that's what is now motivating you. Let me warn you, though. Pain stands waiting for you around every corner. You've got to stand up to it just like David did to Goliath. If you do not, you'll be torn asunder by it. There is no escape from that which reside in your heart. Confront it!" stated the old-timer, emphatically.

The old man turned and walked away from Gabe. He watched him creep off towards the front of the bus. The long nappy, gray hairs of his head and beard seemed to glisten in a halo as he ambled along. He carried a long knotty, walking stick. His feet were clad in a pair of well-used Converse tennis shoes. Gabe blinked his eyes and the guy was gone. He wondered, *How did that guy get past all of those white people getting off the bus? Where is he now? I don't see hide nor hair of him out on the platform. Who is this guy, a ghost or something? I think I've just had a Twilight Zone experience. I'll just keep him to myself—people will think I'm crazy! But I'll never forget that name, William Griot—old Bill Griot.*

Gabe's attention was diverted by Carl Aims, the bus driver. Carl, a lean, tall, white man with that rawboned appearance typical of some southern whites, stood at the bus doors smiling from ear to ear at all the white passengers getting off his bus. His cheeks were ruddy like the clay in the Fluvanna countryside. His dirty-blond hair was thinning in the front. He wore it in a crewcut. His eyes were blue like the Piedmont Mountains. He wore a dark blue, two-piece, bus driver's uniform, a crisp white Van Hausen shirt and a black bow tie. His shiny, black boots shone as though they had been spit-shined. Gabe thought, *This guy must've spent all night shining his shoes.*

Up until Gabe got ready to get off the bus he thought that Carl Aims was pretty cool. But then cold, hard reality hit him like a ton of bricks.

CHAPTER 2

▼

Standing by the bus doors, Aims was very pleasant towards all of the white passengers getting off the bus. Black porters hurried to get some white people's luggage from under the buses' storage areas and handed that to them as they came up with a claim ticket. Aims even went under his bus to aid some white passengers.

It angered Gabe when Carl Aims quickly removed himself from the bus doors as soon as the first Black passenger exited his bus. Aims got a grimace on his face and then sauntered off towards the ticket office of the bus station. He did not lift a finger to get any of their luggage from under his bus, and even the Black porters just stacked Black people's suitcases up on the terminal's platform, and they had to find their luggage the best way that they could. Gabe knew, *This is the South. They never have forgiven us for not consenting to be their slaves. They're set on punishing us for wanting to be free in every little way that they can. We're paying customers too; but look at Old Aims, he can't even treat us like Human Beings. Look at him— he's like a mad dog, or something! When will this all end? When will they stop hating us? What have we ever done to deserve this?*

CHAPTER 3

▼

Gabe stepped off the bus steps onto the loading platform. The gray surface seemed slick under his feet. The painted concrete seemed like it had been sealed and shined making it look like it had been waxed. Gabe knew that they could not have waxed out there for safety reasons.

People ran and walked everywhere to find the right bus to get them to their next destination the fastest. Most would of course avoid the locals. "Is this an express bus," yelled many of them to waiting bus drivers, standing near buses parked at seven gates. "Yes," said several bus drivers. Many passengers got on those buses. As Gabe looked up at the huge overhang there to protect passengers during inclement weather, his eyes moistened. He tried to force a smile on his dry lips to cover the fact that "a grown man was crying," but failed in his feeble efforts. Here he was, out on his own—now what?

As Gabe lamented, the painted-white ceiling above seemed to reflect images that Gabe's mind conjured up related to the pains churning in his young heart. These pains he wanted so badly to forget and leave behind.

Tears eased down Gabe's dark-brown cheeks as his mind lambasted himself.

What the hell am I doing at this stupid bus station in the first place? Gabe's mind screamed at him. The pains of his past surged up, making his stomach feel like a boiling pot. He got dizzy, grabbed hold of one of the steel support beams of the overhang to steady himself, and leaned his head on it. The ceiling lights seemed to blink in oscillation, like an emergency roadside beacon. Gabe closed his eyes, clutched the steel beam with both hands, and the past gushed up into his consciousness like a psychical geyser. It came up out of its repressed subconscious hiding places like a psychical demon. It sounded off in Gabe's head, crowding out reality, drowning out the noise of the buses' diesel engines, the noisy passengers, and time and space. Loud words boomed in Gabe's mental horizon:

"Segregation! Segregation! and all that that stands for, that's the reason you're hurting inside. That's your problem, boy …" went off in Gabe like a megaton bomb. Only it was just Gabe's emotions exploding. Dread, hate and disgust followed. Gabe beat his head against the beam. He could see himself as a little nut-brown boy playing with his father's hunting hounds, then the Rhode Island Red chickens, and then his momma's cats. He was so happy playing with the animals. But his happiness was cut short. A great big old Black man's hands grabbed him.

"Come here to me, boy!" the giant shouted in his bass-registry voice. "I'm going to wear your little ass out!"

The pains came from everywhere all over his young body as Gabe was pummeled with a switch, kicked, stomped and beaten until blisters formed on his back, legs, and all over his head.

"Momma, help me! Help me, momma!" screamed Gabe. He just laid on the ground too sore to get up and run away from his attacker.

Bertha Owens, a five-foot, plump, deep-ebony, woman, wearing a red and yellow, flowery dress, no shoes, and a red bandanna on her head, came running to her wailing child. She scooped Gabe up in her loving arms. The warmth of her embrace somewhat soothed Gabe's wounds.

"I done told you about running between me and that boy, Bertha, when I'm correcting him," spurted out of Allen Owens' mouth after a squirt of tobacco juice. The muscular mill hand clad in his blue, denim, overalls, brogans, and plaid shirt, was snorting at Bertha and her son like a bull that had just served a cow.

Bertha knelt on the ground beside her whimpering only-child. She cried too. "Lord, Lordy-Lord!" she prayed. "Help us all! Save Al."

Allen Owens slapped her one wallop to show her who was boss. He left them outside, sauntering away like a prizefighter who had just won a great match. The Oaks, Poplars, and Pine trees surrounding the modest home of the Owenses, witnessed a little wind in their upper-branches. Bertha hugged her little son to her enormous breasts and whispered, "Hush, now. God's going to take care of us. That's His sign up yonder in the branches of them trees. The wind is a sign of the Holy Ghost, Gabe. God knows what we're going through. He's going to fix it after-while," whined Bertha with a sigh.

It had all gotten started, like it had most times, when Allen came home from work and Gabe hadn't gotten back from the spring fast enough. The evening was cool and Gabe played at the branch that led away from the spring into the woods a little too long, lost track of time. Allen wanted a fresh, cool, drink of water immediately after he got home from work. He caught Gabe on his way from the spring with two, two-gallon, galvanized buckets of water. Allen lit-into his little son.

In Gabe's ears were the sounds of his mother's sobbing for herself and her son. His father's voice permeated his mind, his soul, to the depths of his being with, "I got to bow down to segregation all day long at that concerned mill. I can't do a God-bless-it thing about it! I ain't going to allow my wife and child to disrespect my wishes at this house on my place. I'll kill both of you, first," yelled Allen Owens.

The bloodshot eyes of his father, and the foam that formed at the corners of his mouth as he ranted and raved, had been burned into Gabe's memory. The image of his father kicking his mother as she laid prostrate on the ground was also there too. The feeling of, *I wish I could kill that mad dog,* was the only trump card Gabe ever played. That is why the hate and disgust got buried down deep within his psyche.

"I'm the man in this-here house. You all better get that straight in your minds. Don't neither one of you ever buck against me," bellowed Allen, then he wiped his brow with his big hands. He delivered a final blow to Bertha, who just wept and stayed on the ground, the floor, the whatever!

It was impossible for Gabe to sleep after one of Allen's outrages. On this day, after Gabe had reached the age of thirteen, he asked his mother, "Why don't you leave daddy? Why do you stay with a man who don't love you or me?"

Bertha wept softly while answering her son. "Gabe, where we going? Ain't none of our relatives, or friends, got it any better. Might as well stay and make-do."

She walked away from Gabe with a look of utter sorrow on her face.

Even though Bertha had kept their little home spotless, Gabe could still hear his father yelling at her, "You keep this place looking like a pigpen," because the house had to look like it had just been scrubbed everyday that Allen came home. Betha had to rip and run to get it that way. Her failure meant a big fuss and sometimes a slap in the face, or maybe a beating. Allen was never satisfied.

Bertha made draperies and curtains just as pretty as those Gabe saw in the Sears' wish-book, but Allen scoffed at them as though Bertha's efforts went for nought. Making those draperies was hard work for Bertha, the house had windows on all four sides of it. Times were that Gabe would try to help his mother, but to no avail. There just was never enough hours in a day to get the house spic and span and the draperies and curtains looking like new every-live-long-day. Not to mention the way Bertha had to clean the wood heater and cooking stove, sometimes weeping and singing hymns as she worked as fast as she could. Gabe went into his room some days to just cry for his mother. He hated the way his father treated her.

One evening Allen called for Gabe. "Come here, boy. I'm going to tell you something," said Allen. The muscles of his face twitched as he spoke. "Come on in this front room. Sit over yonder on that end chair. I'm go tell you like it is."

Gabe wondered, *What the hell is it now? The house looks fine. He got his cool drink. What else does he want?*

"Boy, let me tell you this-here. I know you think things are hard around here. I know you believe I'm the devil-on-wheels. But I'm here to tell you, I ain't," said Allen, with a facetious smile across his hairy unshaven face. Gabe frowned at him.

"It's that segregation that's on my back, boy. You're fifteen. Soon you're going out on your own and then you going to know what I be talking about. I stays mad, Gabriel. I stays mad as hell. I know it don't make no sense for me to be taking all that out on you and Bertha, but sometimes I just can't help it. Boy, one of these days, you're going to do the same God-bless-it thing," said Allen, then he lit his corncob pipe. Seems as though his eyes were about to drop a tear down or something. That was something Gabe had never seen before. It shocked him.

"Daddy, I never contradicts you. But this time I have to. I'll never take out any of that stuff you call 'segregation' out on my wife or children. The bad in the world will make me closer to them, not drive me away from them," Gabe dared to answer his father back.

Gabe saw Allen sobbing, crying out loud, almost choking on each sob. He had his big old hands up to his face. "Go on out of here, Gabe," shouted Allen. Gabe lost no time sprinting on out the front door.

The very next day, the harassment got started again. It just went on up until Gabe was about to turn sixteen. He'd developed into a six-one, 130-pound, bean pole. On this day he confided to Bertha his mother, "Momma, I'm too big for daddy to be hitting on me like he likes to do. I'm going to stop him one day with that shotgun in there, I swears!" Gabe almost yelled, pacing back and forth around the kitchen table. He went on out onto the back porch. Bertha came out there and sat on one of the two rough benches on the porch.

"Gabe, honey," Bertha whispered, after a long sigh, "listen to your momma, son. Listen good."

Bertha folded her hands in her lap. Her big, beautiful, African eyes, filled with tears that did not roll down her cheeks, waiting for a more opportune moment.

She rarely looked anyone, including Gabe, in the eyes, being that she was so shy and self-conscious, but she stared at her son now earnestly and directly.

"Baby, your father's a handsome man. He's a hard-working, good provider. Even though he's been at that saw mill down yonder in Columbia most of his life, he's still just a low-paid mill hand. All them white men what came in after him got their training from Al. He even had to train some to be his boss," came out of Bertha, surprising Gabe. She was usually quiet, even when Gabe thought she should've spoken up.

"Yeah, I know, momma. That ol' segregation kept him down. I've heard that one often enough," allowed Gabe, a note of sarcasm ringing through his immature voice.

"There's a lot more to it than that, darling," Bertha interrupted Gabe. "Your father was the smartest boy in his class at West Bottom grade school. Finished the fifth grade with all A's. He went to Stage Junction Negro Elementary and graduated from the eighth grade with all A's. The Owens family didn't have enough to send him to Hampton, or even to Virginia State. So, Al had to go to work at the Dobbs Brothers Mill long before he was actually old enough to. He started as a water boy.

Worked his way up to a saw hand, then on to the plainer. All the time, his wages stayed the same as all of the other colored mens, as low as possible."

Gabe had heard that one before too. "Momma, why didn't he just up and take us up North, or maybe to somewhere else? He didn't have to stay around here. He must've liked it, or something!" suggested Gabe.

"No, baby. In the 30s and 40s, it was the same everywhere for colored folk. Weren't no better nowhere Allen could've gone. He knew that. A mule had kicked Al on his knee, making him unfit for military duty. So many young mens went into the Army during World War II to better they-selves. Got GI Bill benefits. They built homes, opened restaurants, dance halls, and got started farming. Not Al. The mill was like his prison. He hated that, but stuck it out," said Bertha in a very sorrowful voice. "Gabe, he felt trapped. He took up with me …"

The look on Bertha's face almost brought tears to Gabe's eyes. "Momma, don't say 'he took up with you.' You're not a head of cattle, a sow, or a laying hen. You're a beautiful, Black, woman …"

Bertha's eyes eased a tear down her ebony cheeks. "Gabe, I was twenty-one when your father started looking at me. I had never been with another man. Most thought I was too black. I had short nappy hair. Some said my eyes was too big, and my nose, and my head. Al's the only man who ever paid me any attention at all. I liked him from the start. My parents and him got together and we all decided Al and I ought to get married. I was glad," said Bertha with a broad smile on her face.

Gabe's face showed a deep and sad frown. "What, momma? You sound as though you're proud to have been put on a auction block like the slaves back in the day. It was because you must've not loved yourself, momma," rushed out of Gabe's mouth.

"When everybody around you tells you that you're ugly, Gabe, how will you be able to not believe it? A handsome man wanted me. Al wanted me. I couldn't turn him down for no reason. I made up in my mind that I'd go through thick and thin with that man. I married him right away. Shortly after that, you came along. Al was strict and angry at the world from the start. We had our tender moments though. He wanted more children, but after a difficult time bringing you into the world, I was left barren. That was just another big disappointment for Al. He figured to measure his worth as a man by the number of children he could sire. I'm so sorry about that," whined Bertha.

"Momma, that's not your fault. Blame God, or someone like that. It's not something that you did to yourself," shouted Gabe.

"Don't never blame God! I know it's not my fault. But I just want you to see some of the things I believes is turning around in Al's mind," said Bertha.

"Momma, you still could've left! …"

"Gabe, I didn't have nowhere to go. Momma and daddy are dead. Ain't no other man going to take me in with a ready-made family. I had to stay with Al. Besides, I didn't want to leave. Most of the time, Al's good to me. He just like me to clean too much," chimed Bertha.

"Why, momma? What's your explanation for that?" Gabe almost screamed.

"Gabe, white folks always saying that we coloreds are '*dirty Niggers*' and that stuck in Al's guts. He swore nobody would be able to truthfully say that he was one of them dirty, big-N's. That was why he made us clean so much; and, that is why he spent so much money buying materials so that I could make curtains and draperies. He was just afraid, Gabe," said Bertha with a sigh. "I love your father no matter how many faults he got. And, I admit that he got a many. So, you see, I'll never leave him."

Gabe's eyes were downcast. "I guess, it'll be better if I left, than …"

"No, baby. I don't want to lose either one of you! But … I agree that it might be best if you left before you did that … what … you said."

"Momma, I'll put up with daddy until this June. Then I'm going to leave. I don't want to leave you behind, but I can see that you'll never leave daddy.

You're just afraid to, just like he's afraid to leave that mill job. School will close in June, and I will be leaving right away."

Bertha jumped up and seized her tall, skinny son. She hugged him with all of her might. He hugged her back and they both cried.

"Hang in there, Gabe. You got to hang in there, okay?" said Bertha.

"I'm going to, for you momma. You're all I got in this world. I got eleven-years of schooling, too. I might be able to finish some day on my own. But right now, I got to move on. Daddy will never change, neither will I," shouted Gabe.

"Yes, you're just alike. Both of you are stubborn as hell! ..."

The day approached when it was time for Gabe to depart. He collected a couple of changes of clothing in a paper bag, along with some socks and underwear, and an extra pair of Converse tennis. He kissed Bertha, this early morn, and was ready to depart, when a very surprising thing happened.

"Gabe, son, I want to say a couple of things to you before you go out in life. I know you don't understand a lot of things, right now," said Al with a mournful tone to his otherwise raspy, grating, voice.

"Daddy, you've surely waited too late to start talking to me about anything. I can't imagine what you've got to tell me now," answered Gabe, sardonically.

"If you'd just listen for a minute or two. Here goes. Gabe, you have no idea what's out there. I've protected you all these years. You ain't never been hungry. You have always had all the clothes you need. I got all of your schoolbooks and stuff. You did a bang-up job up yonder at S. C. Abrams high. You could end up at Virginia State, Norfolk State, or even Howard University. You're smart enough," preached Al.

"Daddy, there's just one problem," shouted Gabe.

"What's–what's that?" asked Al.

"You, daddy. I can't stand being around you another day. I'd just as soon starve to death," shouted Gabe.

Allen stood up and approached Gabe like he might hit him or something.

"Boy, you don't have to sass me. You just tall, but you ain't tall enough to get snotty with me. Certainly not in my house," Al shot back at Gabe.

Gabe was madder than ever. "I'm leaving here daddy to keep from killing you!" screamed Gabe.

"Go on, then! Get out! But one day you'll come to know what's going on when segregation stares you in the face, gets in your way, and bind you up like a roped cow at a rodeo. You'll get to be just like me. I tell you–you'll become just like me!" shouted Al.

Al and Gabe stood eyeing one another until Bertha got between them.

"Gabe, come on, I'll walk you to the bus stop. The old bus will be along any moment, now, son," pleaded Bertha.

Allen went over to his easy chair, got out his corncob pipe, lit it up and puffed away. Tears eased down his cheeks as he allowed out of the corner of his mouth, to his departing son, "Boy, take care of yourself, and remember you always got a home you can come back to."

Tears came to Bertha's eyes just then, and Gabe had to fight back the tears. He wondered, *Why daddy had to wait all these years before showing any compassion? Why he had to wait until I hated him bad enough to want to never see him again? I'll never understand daddy–I don't reckon.*

It was a sunny morning, outside. Gabe and Bertha walked down the graveled road in silence. Their silence was broken by the diesel engine of the bus. As the bus approached, Bertha blurted out, "Why do it have to be such a beautiful morning, since my only-child is going out into the world, Lordy-Lordy?" she moaned.

The bus pulled up, its doors swung open. Bertha wiped her bloodshot eyes, and just as fast tears spilled out of them again.

Gabe tore loose from his mother, ran up the bus steps, stopping to pay the fare. He handed the driver sixty-cents. "To Charlottesville," he said, nervously.

Carl Aims glanced at him out of the corners of his eyes, "Y'all load from the back, now, you hear?" he uttered.

In Gabe's mind he thought, *This twisted-looking, thin-lipped cracker, I wish I could jam my fist into his mouth to wipe that crap-eating grin off of his arrogant face. I can see the hate for me in his eyes.*

As Gabe ambled on to the back of the bus he considered the fact, *Ah-huh, this is that 'segregation' that daddy harped about all of my nearly sixteen years. The back of the bus. I hate the thought of it. It is the reason I got so many ass-whippings for no good reason!* Then the bus pulled off and bumped Gabe down into a seat in the very back of the bus. He looked out the bus' windows to see his mother throwing kisses at him, with tears streaking down her cheeks like a river. Gabe hung his head and squinted his eyes to fight back the tears.

CHAPTER 4

▼

In the back of the bus, Gabe watched the rolling hills covered with thick foliage go swishing by as the bus churned its way up Route Six. He saw Crape Myrtles coming into bloom, making the countryside seem like a variable flower garden. Hydrangeas mixed in with Rose bushes and Irises caused Gabe to wonder at Nature. He surmised, *It is not just one color that Nature chose to convey beauty, but an unending mix of different colors.*

Gabe's attention got diverted from the beauty and wonder of the countryside by the chatter he heard in the back of the bus. One middle-aged rotund woman with her speckled-gray hair up in a bun, had jowls that hung down from fat. She was working away on chewing gum, like someone eating food. Her tan nose had a large, black, mole on it the size of a raisin. Her very full-lips were smeared with too much bright-red lipstick. She was stuffed in a gray maid's uniform all 200-pounds of her, on about a five-foot frame. Embroidered on the left breast-pocket of her dress were the words "U-V-A *janitorial services,*" in red letters.

Gabe marveled at the total amount of rouge she had smeared on her cheeks on top of pancake makeup. Her big, walnut-shaped eyes were accentuated with eyeliner and mascara. She was sitting beside another woman wearing a similar uniform. This one had a pink-brown complexion, with more pink than brown. Her silky, brown, hair was in huge curls that shined. Her thin nose, lips and ears, and her greenish-gray eyes made her very much resemble a white woman. She kept a facetious smile on her face. She was long and lean.

The fat woman squinted at the lean one and allowed, "Dora, I done heard-tell, and it's all over the news these days, something fixing to happen here in the southern states, directly." Her voice was deep and throaty.

"Yeah. Them white politicians they afraid of our Dr. Martin Luther King, Jr., Lucy," the lean maid replied with a slight bit of glee to her squeaky voice. She lightly clapped her hands with a little chuckle.

The fat maid smiled. She let out a chuckle that made her fat jaws roll.

"Yes sir, I bet Mr. King done upset a whole lot of them white boys, all over the South and the North, too!" chimed Lucy. She smiled from ear-to-ear when she noticed that a few nearby whites looked her way annoyed as hell.

"I hope the colored folk will watch out for him, though, Dora, because that Reverend is my heart," said Lucy.

"Me too, Lucy. I swear to God and hope to die—I don't want to see nothing at-toll happening to that beautiful man. And he's so smart too, girl!" said Dora. She crossed her heart with her right hand.

Lucy shook her head in agreement. They both laughed like schoolgirls.

"Lucy, because of that man's efforts, I'spects we're going to have our freedom one day, soon. I bet it'll be sooner rather than later. He ain't waiting on no white folk to do it for us. He's demanding it, now, honey. That's what I like about that righteous man. I love him!"

Gabe's attention got diverted to a well-dressed, Black man, built like a wrestler, wearing a two-piece black suit, a black fez with small, yellow, half-moons and stars printed all over it, a black-silk bow tie over a white-silk shirt, and black patent leather shoes. The Muslim was at least six-foot tall. His black eyes were set in a rough, brown forehead. He looked narrowly at the maids, moving his shaved head back and forth as each one spoke. At times, his tapered lips grimaced, and his broad nose flared. He shook his head at the conversation going on behind him in the next aisle. He raised his big hands. "Sisters! Sisters! Sisters!" the Islamic-looking guy called out. He had a deep, mellow voice.

The two maids looked over at him and both got little annoyed smiles on their faces.

"I'm sorry to have to disillusion you, but the fact is, Dr. King—as brilliant as he is—will never be able to do much against the evil forces of *The Great Satan, America!*" the Brother preached, balling up his fists and gesticulating with his massive hands. The two maids looked embarrassed. It seemed as though the gentleman was talking loud enough so that everyone on the bus had to hear him.

"Let Allah be praised! You see, dear sisters, we must free ourselves from the oppressive-grip of the white devils over here in America. We have to stand up and defend ourselves like men. That's the only way we're going to prevail against this wicked oppressor over here. Praise Allah!" The muscles of the Muslim's jaws danced and twitched as he preached. The veins of his neck stood out, and his lips were puckered with anger.

Dora and Lucy looked at each other with great puzzlement. "Who the hell is this guy?" whispered Dora.

"I-on-know!" said Lucy, with a shrug of her shoulders.

The man had Gabe's undivided attention. Then the Brother preached on.

"We lost, found, Black people of the Tribe of Shabazz must return to the Religion of Islam, that our forefathers worshiped in before they were hauled off to America in chains in the holds of slave ships," exhorted the Muslim Minister. He shouted now like a Baptist preacher, clapping his hands for emphases.

Lucy looked hard at Dora, both were astonished and a little annoyed at being preached at so hard by a minister they did not understand.

Gabe wondered, *If Islam allowed Black people to become enslaved, why would free Black people want to embrace it? I don't know about this one!*

The Muslim Minister spoke in a quiet voice now as he encouraged, "You all must listen to the young minister who's traveling all over America and building Mosques everywhere, spreading the Good News of deliverance to the Original Man in this world, the Black Man! He will show you the way back to greatness after the teachings of Wallace D. Muhammad and the Honorable Elijah Muhammad. These are our modern day Prophets. Hear them! Embrace their teachings! And, we will overcome the stranglehold 'The Great Satan' has on all of us. The time is at hand!"

His voice rose in volume till it annoyed the white passengers and they started loudly mumbling. Many turned their heads in the direction of the Muslim Minister and gave him a dreadfully dirty look.

Gabe didn't know whether to feel very good or terribly embarrassed at what he had heard and seen. Then another person spoke up.

A cream-colored woman, small of statue, with reddish hair, she wore in a straight-ish Afro, got excited. Her pink cheeks blushed as she rolled her blue eyes, puckered her thin, parched lips, with no trace of makeup on her pale face, to squeal at the Muslim Minister, and all who were seated in the back of the bus.

"Y'all, we don't need no militant nor nonviolent movements in America that'll do nothing but just stir up trouble. We all got it pretty good over here in America. Don't make no never mind how we came over here. We're all in the same boat now. Just look at Africa, Asia, and Latin-America, and you'll see millions of peoples starving to death," said the little lady, blinking her eyes as she spoke.

"We Blacks got it very good over here in America–a lot better than Blacks got it over yonder in Africa. Least we can make a living and raise a family. They can't do that over yonder. I wouldn't want to go live nowhere else. We got to be grateful to God for all of His blessings. We need to do our work and be quiet, that's what I say," said the little lady, wearing a nurse's aide green and white uniform. It mimicked a nurse's uniform. She shuddered as she talked rapidly in sort of a monotone. She had a southern drawl.

"I think white folks done treated me and us Black folk mighty good, if you ask me," whined the little nurse's aide.

When the little lady finished speaking, Gabe could feel the angry silence in the back of the bus. Everybody stared at the little lady, then everyone's voice was going at the same time, so that Gabe couldn't make out anything they were saying.

The bus stopped at this nook and that cranny, filling up with people of all colors who paid their fares, found a seat in the back of the bus or in the front, putting their bags overhead, or Aims got out to put their luggage under the baggage compartment.

The smell of cigarette smoke, and just plain o' B-O, soon dominated all other odors on the bus. Then, Gabe saw little cottages, some fine brick homes, and some with just wood siding, as the bus rumbled up Monticello Avenue to East Water Street. Gabe's eyes widened as he saw stores with huge neon signs, and plate glass windows, reaching up two or three stories high. These increased and grew more congested together as the bus came nearer to the bus terminal. The traffic and noise also grew in intensity, along with the stench of gasoline fumes, mixed with stale food odors, and the putrid smell of burning coal. Soon as the doors opened, the odors came in and built up to unbearable levels. Gabe had to gasp for breath. He made his way to the front of the bus. As Gabe finally got off the bus he reasoned, *This city looks a whole lot better than it smells....*

"Young man. Young man, are you all right?" the soft voice of a white lady asked Gabe. She was very pretty, wearing a white nurse's uniform with a blue sweater pulled over her shoulders, and a little cap on top of her blond hair. She smiled showing even pearly-white teeth. Her big, bluish-green eyes sparkled as she looked up into Gabe's Black face. She was shaped like Mae West or Marilyn Monroe. Gabe's thoughts pummeled convention for a second, *This beautiful dish of forbidden fruit is standing so close to me I could almost kiss her; but it'll be the kiss of death for me!*

"You … You seem to be out of it. Are you feeling good? Why were you beating your head against that beam?" the white damsel asked Gabe.

Her cream-colored-complexion with two petite lips, painted rose-blush, almost brushed against Gabe's cheek as she went behind him to massage his shoulders. Her touch aroused deep feelings of longing in Gabe that he knew would be impossible to explore. So he suppressed the very idea. The struggle made his body shudder.

"I guess I'll be all right … just haven't eaten, is all," said Gabe, then he moved away from the white lady before anyone—especially white men—got the wrong idea. He didn't want to end up like the Scottsboro Boys, Mack Parker, or Emmett Till.

"Well, I've got to catch a street bus up to the University where I work. It'll be along any minute now. I'd best be on my way. You take care young man," said the white lady, and she was gone on out in front of the bus station to a bus stop across the street at the corners of Fourth and West Main Streets.

Gabe watched the sexy swaying of her hips as she walked away. She turned and smiled at Gabe. She waved back to him and that made Gabe fretful.

His mind filled with its previous thoughts, *This is what daddy must've meant about that old "segregation stuff." I couldn't say a word to the woman, even though she was flirting for all she was worth. Her name tag had "Mrs. P. Doll" on it, but I could've sworn she was into Black men! Oh, I got to pee! …*

The big, glass, doorways into the bus terminal had the words "White Only" written in white letters on a black background up in the transom area of the doors. A little side door had the words "coloreds only" written on its transom. It was as minimal as it was meant to be.

Gabe entered the terminal through the "coloreds only" doorway. He entered an entranceway that led to a broad area with plush padded seats covered with black and white vinyl, lots of space and ample seating. This area was filled with white people waiting to catch a bus somewhere. Most had some small bit of luggage sitting beside or near them. Some anxiously monitored their watches.

In the middle of this area, Gabe saw a large white counter with red-topped stools. A black menu board overhead listed with white letters, hotdogs at fifteen cents, twenty cents with chili. A hamburger cost twenty-five cents, thirty cents deluxe. French fries were fifteen cents extra. A hamburger platter went for one dollar. It came with french fries and coleslaw. A large cup of soda was fifteen cents, a medium was ten cents and a small was five cents. Looking at pictures of all the food made Gabe very hungry. His stomach growled. When he spied the large moon pies' and chocolate chip cookies' rack, his big guts commenced to choking his little guts something awful. But a huge sign hung over this, too, stating, "Whites Only!"

Gabe's eyes fastened onto a snack stand that had packages of Ritz crackers, and Mary Jane candies, as well as large Hershey bars. Gabe was so hungry, but all of that existed on the "Whites Only" side.

A large black arrow painted on the beige tile on the floor pointed to the "coloreds only" area. Gabe headed towards that area. He first noticed that he was in a very cramped place. There were no seats and no lunch counter. There was standing room only.

The weary Black travelers had their bags with them and some appeared to be huddled around in a bunch like Gabe had seen cattle doing in the fields. When their buses arrived, they had to hustle through the terminal passing by whites, who were seated leisurely in booths or at tables, or out in the spacious waiting area. The whites took their time eating their food, they laughed and joked with each other and appeared to be having a glorious time. When the Blacks got out on the platform, the porters even ignored them until all of the whites had been served. Some had to tag their own bags because the porters just handed them the tags and walked off.

Then Gabe spied the other menu board. A hotdog was fifty cents, sixty with chili. A hamburger was seventy-five cents, and one-dollar-and-fifty deluxe. Cheeseburgers were eighty-five cents, and cost one dollar more deluxe. An order of french fries cost thirty-five cents. That was the entire menu. No drinks. Blacks were required to order through the dirty busboy window where dirty dishes were returned from the white side of the place and placed in a bus tray to be later washed. All orders for Blacks were to go. There was no place for them to sit down to eat a sandwich or a meal. So most understandably ordered nothing. Gabe had to pee real bad. "Let me go on up them stairs to the men's room," he whispered to himself. Up the stairs, the contrast between the new-looking white side, and the dirty, inferior "coloreds'" side was striking and very defeating to Gabriel Owens. He thought, *I'm glad I don't have to wait for no connecting buses in this crap hole!*

Once he climbed up to the top of the stairway, Gabe saw a big, brown, door that had the words, "White Ladies," painted on it with bold, black-edged, white letters. It stood on the left side of a hallway not far from another door with similar letters that said, "White Gentlemen." Far down the hallway near the end of it was another little brown door with small black letters depicting, "colored girls," and a similar one next to it with "colored boys," written on it.

Gabe smelled the sanitary odors of pine sol, bleach, and a hint of ammonia, as he walked past the "white" restrooms. The closer he got to the "colored" restrooms, he noticed that the scent of urine filled the air. When Gabe finally arrived to his inferior destination, he had to pee real bad, so that made him rush through the door. He saw two urinals on one side of the four walls, and across from those were two stools enclosed by ragged stalls. On a third wall was one nasty hand sink.

Long lines of prancing men protruded from each urinal. The stalls cost five cents, so only those with that amount of change could use those. Some mercifully held the door for an old man or two. Gabe could barely hold his pee. Then he found himself up at one of the urinals that had a little stream of urine running from it, just like the other one had. When Gabe let-loose, it hit the wall behind the urinal from the sheer pressure of it spurting out all of a sudden. But Gabe felt like, *Ah-h-h, that feels so good, o' man!*

When Gabe stepped back from the urinal, he saw that the stream of piss flowed into a drain in the middle of the floor. That was where the smell came from. Some urine had also puddled on the floor. Then the place filled up with a rotten scent. One like rotting potatoes. As Gabe turned to walk away from the pee on the floor he slipped and almost fell. Good thing he didn't. A huge "turd" was curled up on the floor, and Gabe would have landed right on it.

Then Gabe spied an old man that seemed to be in his sixties. He was the one that had pushed by Gabe to get off the bus in a hurry. He was so well dressed, Gabe expected a lot more out of him. It was he that was pulling up his pants after letting it go right on the floor. Gabe twitched up his nose at the scent, and the old man looked like he might cry.

"Sonny, I'm sorry," the old guy whined. "I'm just too old to hold it like you young bucks can."

Gabe just backed away from the filthy, stinky, scene, feeling sorry for all who had to be subjected to such filth in a public restroom at a bus station. When Gabe decided he'd go to the sink to wash his hands, he encountered a long line protruding from it. Some old men were using it as a urinal. Then two of them wet their pants.

I might as well forget about washing my hands! thought Gabe. He turned and headed for the door. The stench of the place started to bring up slimy spittle up Gabe's throat. He almost gagged. Then it happened. Vomit gushed up his throat and out of his mouth. It splattered on the floor, leaving a sour taste in Gabe's throat and mouth. He just wanted to get out of there!

Three young men, one a little older than the rest, came bursting into the john. They all wore tan khakis, high-top, white, Converse tennis and different colored, turtleneck, shirts. They looked tough to Gabe, like bad dudes. His mind was off the smell in the place for a second, as he sized up the "Popeye The Sailor" types. *Man, these guys are built up to the hilt. All of them look like professional boxers, or something. I wouldn't want to fade them.*

He watched the guys suspiciously as they ditty-bopped to the center of the terrible smelling toilet. All of them had their hands on their hips confidently asserting their machismo-ism. Gabe's eyes fixed on the one that could be in his mid-to-lower twenties. *This one,* thought Gabe, *was a Black Atlas. He was about six-foot tall. He was mostly all muscles. Must weigh around 200-pounds. He was all bronze-brawn. Even the dude's cheeks were jammed together, compacted, tight muscles, drawn, hard and tough-looking. His light-colored eyes were hawk-like, piercing and fixed in a cold stare that radiated out from him, like some kind of chill-beam, or something. Makes me tremble inside.*

"I'm Bobcat Hinter, you, mo-joe's! I don't give a hump about none of y'all.

All you mo-joe's who don't know about me, I'm here to tell you, watch out suckers, because you're liable to end up on the end of my fists. And, I ain't lying!" the Atlas yelled at the top of his voice. The light flashed off his red Banlon shirt.

Bobcat pimped over to Gabe. An alarm went off in Gabe's mind. *What the heck is he coming over here to me for?*

"Why you eyeballing me, country?" Bobcat said slowly, as he came right over to confront Gabe.

"Sorry, mister. I didn't mean to …" Gabe tried to utter something in his defense. "My name is Gabe. Gabriel Owens."

"Shut up, farmhand!" shouted Bobcat, sneering at a horribly frightened Gabriel Owens.

Bobcat's hands went around Gabe's neck. He found himself lifted up off the floor, dangling by his neck for a second or two. His fear conjured up the thought: *I ain't going to do nothing to get this mad dog madder than he already is.* So, he just stayed in that denizen of brutality, Bobcat's grasp. It felt so good when Bobcat let his feet touch the floor again.

"I'm a fair dude, country. I'm going to give you a chance to be a man or a punk. Right here, right now!" said Bobcat. As all three hooligans stood around Gabe, *Why me!* puffed up in his young mind. He became a little wobble-legged when Bobcat put up his massive fists assuming a boxer's stance, rolling around his fists, at the same time that he circled around Gabe. He had a killer's instinct in his angry eyes.

"Can I just go on about my business, man. I don't want to fight nobody," whined Gabe.

"You ain't going nowhere mo-joe till I say so. Can you dig that, now, country?" shouted Bobcat.

Gabe froze, and his heart beat faster than a weed in a brisk summer wind. His eyes widened, his mouth was as dry as a desert's floor, and his saliva felt like powder in his mouth. *I didn't do nothing to deserve this,* whined Gabe in his heart.

One of the other young toughs, who was built just like Bobcat, only he was wearing a green Banlon shirt, stepped forward to confront Gabe. Gabe noticed that he was a little shorter than Bobcat by about a-foot and some-inches. His face was not as tough-looking as Bobcat's. As a matter of fact, he was actually smooth-looking and was more a baby-faced type. His nose was flat like it had been broken before. He had a relatively small nose, beady little black eyes, and thick, pink lips on an orange-colored face. He had bigger feet than Bobcat's. Looked like he wore over a size twelve. He had those same massive fists, though, just like Bobcat's. He was just as cocky and looked like he was ready to thump on a dude at any moment.

One strange thing that caught Gabe's attention was, the dude had starched-creases in his khakis. That made the tan-coloring of them standout. His Banlon must've been made of pure silk, because it shined or glistened or something. The dude's Converse tennis were spotlessly clean. He wore a little black derby on top of his large head that exposed very wavy, close-cropped, brown hair. What was even stranger, was that the guy had three college rings on his fingers that Gabe doubted he could legitimately claim. This guy didn't at all look like the college type.

"All right, you pig-skinners, I hope you heard what my walk-partner ran down to you. I hope you can dig where he's coming from. If you can't dig-on his rap, up-you! You all can sell us some wolf-tickets and try to throw-down like Joe Louis, understand me? But I'm going to knock you out—got that! I'm good with these hands, everybody knows that! You may as well come on out your pockets on your own. Don't make me come after you. Can you dig it?" shouted this other Black Atlas. The men in the place all trembled, they were scared to death.

The lump of fear in Gabe's throat got bigger and bigger. It was too hard to swallow. He wanted to run, but he was too scared to move. The overhead lights flickered, and in came an old janitor. He was carrying a shiny shovel, and went immediately over to the pile on the floor, scooped it up, unlocked one of the stalls, plopped the stuff into a stool, flushed it, smiling as he did so. He went back out the door, came back in with a mop that smelled strongly of disinfectant, that he used to scrub the spot where the human waste had once rested. It didn't seem like a big deal to him. The hooligans were quiet while the old guy performed his duty. The smell of pine sol mixed with the funk, but made it a little more bearable to Gabe.

Most of the men squeezed out of the door behind the janitor. They left Gabe standing in the middle of the floor petrified from fear. The hoodlums stood around Gabe all but blocking him in. Gabe wondered, *Why are they staring at me like that?* His nervousness caused his teeth to chatter like they did when he was chilly.

The one wearing the green Banlon smiled at Gabe, showing yellow-teeth. "Look, little country dude, I'm Bubbles Quayles, just in case you or any of them mo-joe's want to know. Everybody on the Hill knows who the hell I am. They know I can throw-down with my dukes. We be the greatest thumping dudes on the Hill," bragged Bubbles.

Then the third man, who wore a black Banlon, and that stood at about five-foot tall, with red hair and green eyes, with smooth, tan skin, narrowed his eyes with a little half-smile on his thin lips, then he winked his left eye at Gabe.

"Look, country, I'm James Killeen. Tell you what. If you can drink like a man, then we'll treat you like a man. Bobcat, don't hit him. Let's see if he can hang with the home-boys," said James.

Bobcat dropped his boxing guard to Gabe's great relief. All three roughnecks got into a little chuckle. James had a fifth of Old Forester whiskey still sealed. He popped the seal, and twisted off the top in one quick motion. The top fell down onto the nasty floor. Gabe figured that they wouldn't have any more use for that top. But he also wondered how they were going to down that fifth, just like that, too?

"Gabe, dude," allowed James, "If you can drink liquor like a man, then you got my respect. If we respect you, homes, we'll let you walk out this john like a man. Now, is that crap cool or what?" said James, smiling at Gabe, but looking dead into his nervous eyes.

Bobcat took a, "Glup! Glup! Glup!" drink out of the liquor bottle. He didn't frown or grimace. Just knocked her down. He laughed and handed the bottle to Bubbles and he did likewise; then James hit it the same way. It was Gabe's turn next. The home-boys almost couldn't hold back their laughter.

Gabe had never drank liquor right out of the bottle all at once like the guys standing before him. He hated the taste of it too much. To socialize, he'd mixed a little liquor with a whole lot of soda pop before sipping it slowly. He had no idea how this was going to go. He took the bottle in his shaky hands.

"Take a big hit of that 100 proof booze, dude," bellowed James in a bass-sounding voice.

Gabe turned the smelly liquor up to his innocent lips, trembling as he did so, and tried to gulp down a huge swallow of the brown liquid. Down the hatch it went.

"I can't breathe! … My guts are on fire! …" Gabe managed to blurt out.

His stomach was burning and in knots from the sudden assault of a big drink of liquor. The booze bounced right back up his throat, in a big gulp just as he had swallowed it. He tried hard to re-swallow it. His nose filled with it. Tears ran from his eyes down his cheeks. With all of his might, Gabe re-swallowed the liquor again. He held her down despite his stomach's objections to the contrary. He coughed like he was gong to be strangled, but he held on to his liquor.

James, Bubbles and Bobcat laughed as loud as they could and slapped hands with each other. Seemed like to Gabe, they enjoyed that spectacle too much.

James patted Gabe on his back. Gabe had big tears running down his cheeks from the liquor. He wiped them off with a quick swipe of his hand. Each one of the dudes came and shook Gabe's hand.

With a smile on his tough face, Bobcat slapped hands with Gabe. "From now on, dude, you're one of our walk-partners. There ain't no dudes on the block who know who you're with will ever lay a hand on you. You're part of the Crew that rules the Hill. Just tell them you're one of the Bobcat's Crew. You down with that, Gabe?" said Bobcat.

"Yeah, man—I reckoned," said Gabe in a whisper, still out of breath a little.

Bobcat, James and Bubbles lined up to shake Gabe's hand one at a time. After he had shook each of their right hands, they all gave him a brotherly hug. Bobcat smiled like he might have been looking at an adoptive brother. His eyes beamed a confidence usually found in military drill sergeants after their new recruits graduated.

"These-here be my main men," said Bobcat, pointing to a chubby James, and a too neat Bubbles. "We been walk-partners from way back to kindergarten. We all grew up on the Hill. Been over there all our lives. Probably go die there one day. One thing you got to remember is, we be thumping mo-joe's, Gabe. We'll jump on a sucker any time of the day and stomp him into bad health, if we got to. We don't be playing. You digging where I'm coming from?"

"Sure' nough," answered Gabe.

"We're known all over the Hill by all of the righteous-thumping home-boys. Most of them is in my Crew. That's why nobody screws with me, 'The Bobcat,' because their butt can't carry the load I'm a put on it when it's time for payback. You digging this crap! Gabe" said Bobcat.

"I'm digging it. Nobody messes with you and the walk-partners," said Gabe almost overwhelmed by the thought of it all.

"Now, can't nobody screw with you, Gabe, because we like you, country. You're our boy. If anybody tight-legs you, just let one of my Crew know. It'll be all-she-wrote! dig?" chimed Bobcat.

"I'm down with that," said Gabe.

Bobcat gave Gabe a bodacious hand-slapping, Bubbles and James followed.

Bubbles twisted up his lips and uttered, "What kind of name is 'Gabe' anyway? Sounds like something I heard at Sunday School or something."

"It's out of the Bible, man. My moms pinned it on me. Short for Gabriel and whatnot," said Gabe almost sheepishly.

"Well, that's no kind of name for a walk-partner in my Crew, my-man," ushered out of Bobcats tough-looking face. "Man we got to get you a tougher-sounding street name, homes. The home-boys ain't going to respect no name like 'Gabe!'"

"Okay. Shoot!" replied Gabe. "What you going to call me, then?"

"G-man, that's what I feel will be more better," said Bobcat. "What do you think, Bubbles, James?"

"I likes it find," said James.

"Me too," said Bubbles.

"All right, then. From now on Gabe, you are 'G-man,' one of the newest members of my Crew. One of the main things you got to remember is, never rat-out any of the Crew to the cops. That's a death-sentence, brother man. You got that?" said Bobcat.

"I'll never do that–all right!" answered Gabe, feeling a little more confident now that he was going to be accepted and all. His stomach even settled down, although he was hungry as a pregnant sow. The hooligans downed the rest of that bottle of liquor like it was water. They all laughed at the look on Gabe's face. Then, the home-boys headed for the door.

"Bobcat. I hate to ask. But, I need to get something to eat. Can I barrow a couple of dollars, man?" asked Gabe, smiling like a cat that had just eaten the canary.

"I'll be back through here in a moment, home-slice. If you're still up here at the bus station, I'll hook you up, dig?" said Bobcat. The thugs were gone just as suddenly as they had earlier come into the toilet.

Then it dawn on Gabe, *Let me get out of this filthy hole, dag! Look at the size of those roaches coming up out of that drain. Those inside of that empty liquor bottle got to be drunk or something. They ain't moving no more. Can't be nothing worst than a drunk roach. But, all the liquor Bobcat and them drank, they didn't get drunk. I'm dizzy as hell just from the little I threw down. Got to get on out of here.*

Gabe walked along the hallway pass the other restrooms. The door swung open as he passed the white-men's toilet. Gabe saw about four or five urinals and about five or six stalls. There were several hand sinks on one wall so that no way would the place get so full that one would not be available. All of the hand sinks had mirrors up above them. In the "colored boys'" estroom, there were no mirrors. The white tiles were sparkling clean in the "White Gentlemen's" restroom. So much grime had collected on the walls of the other one, until they appeared to be tan. *It's a shame the way white society treats us Black folk! They treat us like animals, so some of us have taken to acting just like we're being treated.* The thought made Gabe feel like crying or something. He headed on down the stairs.

CHAPTER 5

▼

I hope I never see them roughnecks again. They got to be some very violent dudes. Man, I don't think they're good people. They seem to be liquor-drinking, hell-raisers who could actually kill a dude without thinking much about it, thought Gabe as he headed on back down the stairs.

All the buses had gone by the time Gabe got back to the bottom of the stairway. A little group of dudes came in through the Main Street side of the terminal. They collected in the "coloreds only" side of the waiting area. Gabe figured that it was about time for him to get on out of the place and head on up towards the University of Virginia Hospital. He'd heard from Abe Jones that there would be a good chance of him getting hired, especially if he applied for janitor. So, that's what Gabe had a mind to do. He grabbed the stainless-steel handles of the front doors and was bout ready to swing them open when someone called out to him.

"Hold on there, country," shouted a heavyset dude, wearing almost the same clothing that Bobcat and them had on. Several dudes with the fatso had on the exact same get-ups: black khakis, tan Converse tennis, and red Banlon shirts. They were of various heights and sizes. The one speaking to Gabe was definitely another roughneck, or probably from a rival gang. His face was all beat-up looking and scarred. He was very dark-skinned and had his hair conked, fried, dyed, and laid to the side. Gabe was afraid again. "I'm with Bobcat and them," he blurted out.

"So what!" shouted the heavyset dude with a little grimace. "I'm just as much man as any of that Crew is. I ain't studying about nothing that bunch of punks got to say."

Gabe didn't know what to say … so he said nothing.

"You look just like one of them country punks from down in Fluvanna or Louisa, I swear. Got any change in your pockets, sucker?" asked the behemoth.

"No, I ain't got no money," replied Gabe like a little child, with his voice wavering as he spoke, and his knees feeling weak.

"I been down yonder to Hanover Reformatory. Just got out a couple of weeks ago. We used to make faggots out of little scared Negroes like you, country. What you got to say about that?" the black elephant hissed at Gabe.

"I'm a man, dude. I don't go like that. I ain't no fag!" shouted Gabe.

"You're be whatsoever I say you'll be!" answered the Godzilla. He pulled up on the crotch of his khakis, then a sinister smile came over his battle-scarred face.

In just an instance, the freak-show-reject pulled out a switchblade knife and the blade of it flashed, reflecting the florescent lights in the ceiling. His henchman crowded around Gabe to see what he would do.

With the point of the knife on his neck, Gabe swore to himself, *I ain't got no money, and I ain't going to be nobody's guy-girl.* Gabe's blood rushed to his stomach as he contemplated dashing past the overstuffed pervert like black lightning. The thought of taking it in the butt was one of the most frightening thoughts that Gabe ever had on his mind. He would rather die.

"Go head on cut me or something! I ain't got nothing else for you," shouted Gabe.

"Oh-oh-oh! I think you looking to get rough, country. Well–I'm good! I'll put my knife up. Let's see who got the best dukes. I'll duke you to death!" the gorilla exclaimed.

As scared as Gabe was, the fear of losing his manhood made him throw up his fists. "You want to get it on with G-man–then, come on alligator face!" shouted Gabe. He covered up his fear with all of the macho he could muster.

"G-man! That sounds like one of Bobcat's Crew. He must've given you that name. Now, you want to get-it-on with me, Tyrone Smith? Well, let's go, then!" said Ty. "You can't win, country!"

Ty hit Gabe, a one-two-three, punch combination. Gabe staggered back but didn't fall. Fear made Gabe strike back. He hit Ty a couple of cornfield licks with all of his might rolled into them. A knot came just under Ty's right eye. Gabe's bravery shocked Ty. Then Gabe kicked the donkey in the balls. Just then in came Bobcat and his main walk-partners. Ty scrambled up off the floor. All of his cockiness had gone out the door with the rest of his Crew. He was alone in the hands of an unforgiving Bobcat Hinter. Ty had to become a living example of what happened when a dude got the nerve to step-to a walk-partner. That dude had to realize that he had put his life on the line. Before Ty got a chance to utter a word in his defense, Bobcat popped him. Down he went. Gabe backed against the wall.

The lick Bobcat hit Ty with sounded like a wooden plank breaking. Ty was knocked-out cold. Blood oozed out of his nose. Gabe thought, *Oh, man! What a pitiful sight! I think I'm going to run out that door!*

Bubbles and James got between Gabe and the doors. Gabe had to stay and watch Tyrone Smith get the hell beat out of him.

Ty laid on the floor like a dead man, but Bubbles and James took turns kicking the out-of-it dude around in circles. Gabe almost got sick at the stomach when Ty wet his pants and the walk-partners kept on kicking him, laughing as they did so.

These are some cruel cats. How the hell can they stomp another Black man like that? wondered Gabe. Then his father came to mind. On the one hand, Gabe was glad that Ty was no longer able to pester him; but, on the other hand, he was sad because these soul brothers could just about brutally beat one another nearly to death.

More astonishingly, Gabe saw that the bus station attendants had allowed the Negroes to fight it out, with white passengers standing by, some in alarm, and some with glee, as though they were watching a boxing or wrestling match. After a while, and after Ty was a bloody pulp, police sirens broke up the fight. Bobcat headed on out the door, followed by James, with Bubbles bringing up the rear.

Bobcat hollered, "G-man! Run dude. We got to split the scene!"

Gabe followed behind James, outran him, and caught up with Bobcat. They ended up going down Fourth Street. They ran to the heart of Vinegar Hill. Bubbles and James kept on running down Main Street to Vinegar Hill's east end. Bobcat and Gabe came out on the corner of Fourth and Commerce Streets. They got behind Jefferson High School, and stopped near Zion Baptist Church.

"G-man, we can chill-out for a little while up here," said Bobcat. He spoke while gasping for breath.

"What the hell are we going to do, now?" asked Gabe, out of breath too, but staring intently at Bobcat waiting for the answer.

"I don't know what you going to do, but if I was you, I wouldn't go back up to that bus station for a couple of weeks," said Bobcat with a little chuckle, though Gabe didn't see what was so funny.

"I tell you what, G-man. We can fool around until the cops quiet down, then we'll go over to Mary Lou's house. She's one of my righteous honeys. I can put you on her sister. She's around your age, too," said Bobcat, nudging Gabe gently in his side. He winked at Gabe.

Gabe had to wonder, *How can this guy be ready to do-it so soon after knocking some dude out?*

Gabe rolled his eyes in surprise but said nothing.

"G-man. Mary Lou's sister, man, she's a pretty little woman, man. If you want to get down with a hot little honey, she's it. She loves country dudes like you, too, G-man. How about it–want to do it?" said Bobcat.

"Whatever you want to do, Bobcat. It's all right with me. I owe you and the walk-partners a lot. By the way, thanks man," said Gabe, then he slapped hands with Bobcat.

"Ah, G-man, we walk-partners. I'd do the same for any of my boys," said Bobcat.

"What exactly does your Crew do, Bobcat? What sort of junk are you … we, into?" asked Gabe.

"We rip-off junk-pushers. We ain't about pushing dope on our block like those faggots, Ty Smith, and his Crew. We be very militant, homes. Black militants, that's who we be. We be tearing down whitey from the insides out. Hitting the white boy wherever he's showing weakness. Are you digging where I'm coming from?" said Bobcat. He put out his right hand, palm up. "Give me some dap, then, Gabe."

Gabe looked up at the sky before dragging hands with Bobcat, thinking, *I don't really agree with this guy's ideas, but I'm a just go along for right now.*

CHAPTER 6

▼

The time had flown. "Look Gabe, it's getting dark, my-man. Hey, soon, all the joints will be closed. I want you to jive around with me this evening. Country, I believe you're going to have a lot on the ball. In the bathroom at the bus station, we were just fooling around. We would've never hurt you. I spotted you getting off the bus, figured you'd be a good homey, so me and the boys put one over on you. But, I think you'll be all right, country. I want you to get to know the boys on the Hill."

"Bobcat, I'm hungrier than a starving dog. I ain't had nothing to eat since this morning. That's why that liquor you all forced me to drink went right to my head. I ain't got nothing on my stomach. I ain't got no money, neither," said Gabe, with a little fear swelling up in his stomach. A faint, little, cool breeze started to blow up Fourth Street.

"I got you covered, Gabe. Don't worry. Let's go on over to Commerce to Smithy's. We can get us a couple of bull-burgers, man; you know, thick slices of 'loney, with cheese and grilled onions, and lettuce and tomato and mayo, on a sourdough bun," said Bobcat. What he described made Gabe even hungrier.

"Let's go!" shouted Gabe. Bobcat jutted out his hand for Gabe to deliver dap.

Gabe had come to realize, *I'm a have to give or get dap after every major thing, I guess.*

The smell of hotdogs, chili, and hamburgers cooking, french fries frying, cigarette smoke and alcohol hit Gabe in the face as he and Bobcat ditty-bopped into Smithy's Café. The juke box was blasting, "Pain in my heart/Treat'n me so cold/ Where can my baby be/Lord, no-o one knows/…" as Gabe took notice of the limited space in the rectangular-like place, jammed with young people dancing.

32

The soul music touched that place deep down inside of Gabe that made him feel sad, joyful, and sexed-up, all at the same time. Gabe closed his eyes and savored the beat, felt the lyrics, and caught the spiritual jolt emanating from the music. It temporarily took his mind off being hungry. He heard Bobcat order two bull-burgers and a pitcher of draft-beer.

Al Smith, the owner of the place, came over to look carefully at Gabe.

"Is this cat of drinking age, Cat?" the fat dude asked. He got a twisted smile on his puckered lips, blinking his little gray eyes as he spoke, his graying, brown hair was up in what would one day be called a "'Fro." His beige skin was almost ashy. The dude had a neatly trimmed, pimp-styled, mustache, though, and Gabe dug that.

"Well, Al, you sell him a glass of soda pop. Give me a glass–and we're good to go, okay?" said Bobcat with a little wink.

"I don't want to get the cops breathing down my back. I sell that 3-2 beer and all, y'know. But, I got to be careful, man. I don't want to lose my license–you un'erstand what I mean, homes? I don't care about it–but, the cops would like nothing better'n coming down on my place. Un'erstand me?" said Al.

"Yeah, I dig where you coming from, my-man." said Bobcat.

"You all right with me–un'erstand what I mean? I'm old school, homes–me and your dad go way back. You all just coming down the roads we done already traveled. We been cool a long time. You're what's happening nowadays. I'm just trying to maintain, that's all I be doing, young bloods–un'erstand me?" said Al. "I'll go get your suds and soda pop. Got your sandwiches working, too. Coming right on up, Cat. You be cool, now!" He wiped his hands on his white smock.

"By the way, if the little dude takes a sip of your suds, let him do it quickly out of the same glass you're using. Leave the soda pop sit in front of him. That way we can all stay cool, dig where I'm coming from?" said Al.

"Right on," said Bobcat. All three of the men chuckled.

The food came out first, and Gabe gulped his sandwich right down. Bobcat poured a glass of beer and shoved it at Gabe. "You got to gulp her down, G. That's what Al is saying," said Bobcat.

Took Gabe three gulps before he could get it all down.

"G, you got to learn how to drink if you're going to hang with the Crew. We be some alcoholic dudes, now. That's all we do. Takes an ocean to make one of us drunk, dig?" said Bobcat. Al, in his dark trousers, T-shirt and clean smock, smiled.

"I dig," said Gabe.

Gabe started to feel tipsy as the beer slowly came up on him. Bobcat split his sides laughing at how Gabe looked. When Gabe started to feel real warm inside, and his head was spinning a little, he felt sick at his stomach.

"I'm a throw up, Bobcat," said Gabe.

"Let's get on out of here in the air, dude, you'll be all right. Just got to get used to being down with the booze. You'll get the hang of it real soon," said Bobcat.

"Come on G. I'm a take you over to Mary Lou's house down on Third Street. She's my main squeeze. Man, she's what's happening," said Bobcat.

Gabe staggered along behind Bobcat, after Bobcat paid Al for the meal and two pitchers of beer. Al and Bobcat slapped hands, and Al allowed, "Take care of that young blood, Cat. We got to steer them in the right direction, homes. These be some changing times—you with that?" said Al.

"Yeah, I'm cool with that. I dig where you're coming from," said Bobcat.

Bobcat and Gabe arrived at one of the stucco houses on Third Street. All of them seemed as though they were exactly the same to Gabe. They were like shot-gun shacks with their rough-wood porches flat against the ground. No sidewalks existed and the street these houses stood on was barely paved, full of potholes, and big mud puddles. Red dirt was exposed everywhere. These dwellings were all in a row on one side of the street. On the other side of the street, downtown Charlottesville's businesses began. That made that part of Vinegar Hill all the more conspicuous. Bobcat and Gabe stopped at one of the dwellings and Bobcat knocked on the door.

"Come on, Mary Lou, I know somebody's in there. Y'all got to hear me knocking on this door. Hey, Mary Lou! … Mary Lou! It's me, the Bobcat. What's happening?" said Bobcat, raising his voice just a little.

A short gray-headed lady came to the door. Her skin seemed dry and wrinkled like a raisin. Her deep-ebony African features made her appear like a wise woman, but the way she carried herself made her seemed wizened. Her short hair was worn natural. Gabe saw her hands. They were rough, and stubby, with some arthritic twists to her fingers. Those were hard-working hands.

"Who you want to see?" gushed out of the old lady's mouth. "You bad news, boy. Nothing but trouble. And me, Vera Crenshaw's here to tell you," said the old lady. She threw up her hands in protest. "You ought to go way from here and leave Mary Lou alone before you get her in the family way. Boy, you ain't going to take care of no baby. You still living at home yourself," shouted Vera.

"I loves your daughter, Miss Crenshaw. One day we're going to get married. I means well by her. If she gets in the family way, I'll take care of her and the baby," replied Bobcat, plaintively.

"Yeah, I bet!" said Vera. "Just you remember your promise when the time comes, all right?"

Gabe saw that Vera had on a white dress with a black maid's apron over it. On the left pocket of the dress were the words in black, "Charlottesville City Hall."

Mary Lou heard the commotion. "Momma, who's out there? Is it the Bobcat? Is it my man?" a beautiful, smooth-skinned young woman came swishing to the front door. She had a glossy Afro. Her lips were puckered loveliness. Her eyes were like those of the Queen of Sheba. She had all of the feminine beauty depicted in those pictures that Gabe had seen in his social studies books of Cleopatra. When she smiled, it was like gorgeous moonlight. Her breasts were large and protruding, inviting, and naturally jiggling. *This woman is as pretty as Bobcat says she is,* thought Gabe. She wore a pink continental skirt, a white sleeveless blouse, half unbuttoned, and no shoes. Her toenails were painted red as were her fingernails.

"Hi, Cat! Come on in. Don't mind momma. You know how she is. Who's your friend? Bring him on in too," said Mary Lou.

Bobcat kissed Mary deeply and passionately. Gabe wished he could have some of that. Just then, a shorter, and probably younger version of Mary Lou came swishing into the front room. She had on a green continental skirt, and a thin T-shirt. Her breasts strained against the fabric of it like two ground hogs trying to get out.

"This is Gabe, Brenda, Mary. Gabe, meet Brenda and Mary," said Bobcat.

"Hi, Gabe," the two beauties answered. Bobcat started into kissing Mary Lou again. His amorous behavior was soon interrupted by Vera. She had on a little flowery bonnet and a thin gold shawl on her shoulders. "Mary Lou, I want these mens to be gone by the time I get off from over at the Midway Building. You girls today! I swear!" said Vera. She just stood patting her foot for a second or two, then she was out in the night air, heading on out Third to Main Street. She took a shortcut through the businesses on the Hill to the building that housed the City Council, on the corner of Garret and Ridge Streets.

"Cat, let's go on in there," said Mary in a soft, sexy voice, barely above a whisper. "You know why," she cooed.

"Yes, mamma! I know what you be saying," said Bobcat. He picked up the lovely woman, that looked to be in her late teens, up and carried her towards a door to one of the two bedrooms in the house. It had a big old King-sized bed with lion carvings on the head posts in one corner of the room, and a wardrobe closet in the other. Gabe watched Bobcat take Mary to the bed. He turned and winked at Gabe with a lusty smile on his tough face. Mary got up, ran to the door with a girlishly, mischievous smile on her pretty lips, and closed the door quickly. Multiple giggles came out of the room, followed by the creaking of bedsprings. Gabe knew what that meant.

Brenda looked at Gabe and came walking over to him, smiling very seductively at a nervous Gabriel Owens. "What's the matter, country, don't you like girls?" said Brenda, with a sultry lisp to her speech. "Gabe, I want you … to make a woman out of me. I want you to be the man, tonight, country."

"Brenda, how old are you?" asked Gabe suddenly. He had never been approached like that before. He had only gotten started having sex with a girl at school once, then someone was coming and he had to stop and dash out of the cloak room just in time. He had only gotten a little taste of the warm, juicy, place down there. Now, he could have it all, but was scared to move. Didn't know what to do.

"Come on, country, baby. Let me show you how to do it," said Brenda. She pulled Gabe to her. She held him tightly, kissed him by tiptoeing, and put her tongue in Gabe's mouth. He relaxed. They were soon undressed and on the sofa in the front room. Nature took its course! … Such passion. Such red-hot, delicious passion! Young love, or lust, it didn't matter to Gabe. It was the first time he'd gotten all the way with a woman. After about thirty minutes, it was over. It was so wild and furious, that even Brenda, who was experienced, as Gabe found out, enjoyed it.

"Country, I want to see more of you. What do they call you? I know if you're one of Bobcat's boys, you have a cool label. What do they call you?" asked Brenda, in a schoolgirl's way. She caressed his chest, kissed and nibbled his chin.

"They call me G-man, or just G for short," said Gabe, smiling at his naked new girlfriend, still lying beside him. He was nude also. "I'm just sixteen."

"Look, Gabe, I'm eighteen. Got you by a couple of years, but that's all right, if it's all right with you," said Brenda, as she pulled on her red panties, and her skirt next, and then her T-shirt. He didn't see no bra! Got Gabe excited all over again!

A couple of hours had passed. The fun and games were over. Gabe finished putting on his clothes. "I hope we can get together again real soon, Brenda," said Gabe.

"We can G. I work over in Greenbrier out in Albemarle for the Doll family. I babysit their two girls. Their mother works up at the hospital as a nurse. I'm usually off Fridays and Saturdays. We can get together then. Is that all right with you? We can go dancing at the Hall or something," Brenda chimed, looking up into Gabe's smiling face. She kissed him two or three times between words.

"Yeah, that will be good for me. I don't have a job yet, but I'm probably going to be working up at the hospital as a janitor as soon as I can get up there to apply," said Gabe. "That's not all I'm going to do. I'll probably go back to school, soon as I can. I heard that Burley will let me in … least, that's what I got in mind. We can be real tight, Brenda. I don't know no other girls. I don't think I want to after this evening, baby," said Gabe.

"G, I hope you will stick with that. It'll be cool with me. I ain't got no man out there that I can't breakup with. I could learn to love you. You're so sweet. I hope you stay that way. You're so cute, these tramps up here are going to ruin you. I would love for you to be my man, only; but will you be able to do that? Now that's the question," said Brenda, almost whining.

"Ah, Brenda, I'm not all that cute. What we shared this evening means more to me than that. I'm not like some of these guys up here. I ain't meaning to jump from girl-to-girl like a big old bullfrog. I always wanted to find a good woman and stick with her," said Gabe. "Too, the Doll family, you say? I think I met a nurse by the name of P. Doll up at the bus station. She thought something was wrong with me. I had leaned against a beam to get myself together and this white woman started rubbing my back and shoulders. I didn't know whether to run, or what!"

"Yeah, that's Polly. She's one of them, 'white-liberals,' who claims that Blacks and whites ought to get together and let bygones be bygones. Her husband's got a completely different opinion! …" said Brenda, before she was interrupted.

"Come on G, we got to blow this scene, my-man. Old Vera's about ready to get off work. She'll be home real soon, homes. We can cut over to my crib. My pops will be able to get you on, up at the University Hospital. You digging where I'm coming from?" said Bobcat.

"Yeah, I'm with that," said Gabe.

Gabe got one last tongue-kiss from Brenda. She clung to him like she suspected that she'd never see him again. Gabe had to pull away from her.

"G, don't forget where it's at, now," said Brenda.

"Right-on!" said Gabe.

Mary Lou stood in the doorway of the bedroom where she and Bobcat had done it. She had on a green flannel housecoat, but it was loosely buttoned. Gabe saw her full-bush through the view that the unbuttoned area revealed. It turned him on again; but hey, it was time to split the scene–besides, she was Bobcat's girl.

Gabe and Bobcat plodded along the deserted streets past a row of abandoned houses. They appeared to be ghastly to Gabe, like huge claws and gaping mouths, with jagged teeth. The pale moonlight played on the shrubbery in that place, creating ghostly likenesses, resembling phantoms, goblins, and devils, as the wind swayed the over-and-undergrowth in the area, back and forth. The wind howled through the trees making an eerie moan. *What the hell is going on here!* wondered Gabe.

A bent and weather-beaten street sign had the twisted black letters still visible through the rust, "R-A-N-D-O-M R-O-W," making Gabe wonder about that place on Vinegar Hill. *What sort of place was it? Who had lived there? Why was it empty, vacant and undeveloped? Why did it seem so scary?* Bobcat interrupted his thoughts.

A playful punch in Gabe's side was followed by the question, "G, did you get that thing tonight?" Bobcat asked.

He did not want to answer that question. "Well … I guess … yeah," said Gabe slyly.

"I didn't hear no noise, G. Y'all was mighty quiet. I could've heard a rat pee on cotton. What's happening with that?"

"Cat, you and Mary Lou made so much noise you would never been able to hear what me and Brenda was doing," answered Gabe shyly.

"G, you weren't chicken enough to let Brenda talk you out of getting-it-on with her, like a rag-story, or something?" said Bobcat.

"No! Bobcat. We got-down. Don't worry. We did!" said Gabe, annoyed as hell at Bobcat's questioning of him.

"Listen, G. In this town, you got to prove that you are a man in everything that you do. Like any he-man, get as many honeys as possible. Have them all eating out of your hand. Don't fall in love with none of them. The more, the merrier. I got nearly twenty girls I see whenever I can. Mary Lou is just one of them. I think, she knows that. In The Streets of Vinegar Hill, that's how it be, man," said Bobcat.

That sounded so cold and deceitful to Gabe. "I want to find one girl and treat her right, man," he uttered in an almost hoarse voice.

"Right now, you're just coming up out of the country, but one day soon, you'll be just like me, G," Bobcat replied, shaking his head from side to side.

Gabe doubted that he'd ever become the roughneck that Bobcat is.

"Cat, that place we past, 'Random Row,' what's that all about?" asked Gabe.

"G-man, they found a body of a wino, or something, over there. He was supposed to be a teacher, never known to be into alcohol. But this straight-on-up dude had died from alcohol poisoning? Some said that when the Governor closed the schools to prevent integration, and then reopened them, after firing most of the Black teachers, and the dude had lost his job, as most Black teachers did, he drank himself to death. Got to wearing faded jeans, and old flannel shirts. But people say he was smart, though. Was doing some kind of historical research before he was found stiff over at 'Random Row.' After he lost his job as a teacher, he rented a room from my moms, and said he was going to write a book. We still got all of his notes and all. Ain't nobody rented his room since he died. Oh, we live right here, G," said Bobcat.

Gabe noticed that where he stood was a far cry better than where Mary Lou and them lived. Cat and them lived in a part of Vinegar Hill with houses that had boxwood hedges, front yards, screened-in porches, sidewalks, and some houses were even bricked-up. Fourth, Fifth, Sixth, Seventh and Eighth Streets, North-west, were fine and whatnot; but, from Fourth to First Streets, Northeast, houses were some eighty-or-ninety years behind the times. Mary Lou's house had no running water. They had to use an outdoor toilet. Wood was the fuel that they cooked with and heated the house with. They had no electricity, so they used kerosene lamps.

The house they were about to enter had four to five rooms, with two upstairs. It was nice by anybody's standards. *I don't know what is the matter with Cat, man! It ain't cause he came from the poorest of roots,* Gabe pondered the thought.

Before Gabe followed Bobcat on into the house, a lingering question plagued his mind. "Cat, what was the name of the guy they found over on Random Row, dead?"

"Oh, G," said Bobcat, almost whispering his answer, "the guy's name was William Griot."

The realization hit Gabe like a bolt of lightning. *That was the name of that old guy on the bus with the funny-looking walking stick!* went off in Gabe's mind like a shotgun. He figured that it had to just be a coincidence.

Bobcat, seeing the surprised look on Gabe's face allowed, "Hey, G. Don't worry man, he ain't nowhere to be found. They jacked up his stiff and took him straight away to be cremated. Said that he was too badly decomposed to embalm, and whatnot. I doubt that, but y'know? … That's how stuff go down, man."

Gabe whispered to himself, "Oh, man! I done seen a ghost. Just can't be. I don't believe in that stuff. I will never believe in that! …"

He followed Bobcat into the house. Gabe was blown away. He found himself in a spacious front room, with a plush dark-green, wall-to-wall carpet, a brown leather sofa and love seat, with two matching end chairs. In each corner of the room stood tall floor lamps topped by angelic-print lampshades, full of Black

Cherubim, on a gold background, with silver grapevine designed bases. In the middle of the room in front of the sofa, was an African-styled coffee table depicting gorgeous, carved, African figurines all around its rectangular edges. Various African masks stood in the middle of it. Gabe had never seen anything like that front room before in his life. On the walls were paper with scenes showing various animals, such as the elephant, hippopotamus, crocodiles, lions, tigers, zebras, and giraffe in Africa. The pyramids of Egypt were also depicted, as were some of the Hindu goddesses of India.

"Good morning boys," came out of the large kitchen. A mellow baritone voice filled up the early morning. "I know you boys are hungry. You both look like you been prowling the streets most of the night. Ah, to be young again," said the gray-haired gentleman in the kitchen. He chuckled, then flipped over some pancakes he had frying on a portable grill resting on two of the electric eyes of his new stove. Gabe smelled bacon cooking, and saw a pan of scrambled eggs, steaming.

The overhead ceiling light grew dimmer, seemingly, as the bright sunlight came cascading through the little kitchen window over the sink area. Red roses on the blue window-curtains seemed as though they were blowing in the wind as the cool breezes of the early morning flowed through the kitchen. Mr. Hinter filled a big, black coffeepot with water from a faucet over the kitchen sink, scooped a liberal helping of ground coffee beans out of a large bag with a plastic scoop, put that into its percolator, and set the pot on a vacant eye of the stove. The gas water heater sitting in a far corner came on with a loud "puff!" that startled Gabe a little, not being used to modern conveniences.

Gabe took a good look at Mr. Hinter and saw a tall golden-colored man, with a natural smile on his broad face. He had very straight black hair that he had waved in the front of his head. He had those sharp eyes that were so striking about Bobcat. He was smooth-faced with just a hint of a thin mustache. Gabe figured that he kept it trimmed that way. He had the musculature of a wrestler. But had the mild manners of a cultured gentleman.

"You boys, come on in and get something to eat. Junior, bring your boy, he's welcome. Got a plenty. Enough for everybody. Junior, your boy looks like he could really use a meal. Y'all come on," crooned Mr. Hinter.

"Thank you very much, sir," replied Gabe. "Don't mind if I do. My name is Gabriel Owens," said Gabe, extending his hand for a friendly shake.

"Please to meet you, Gabriel. I'm George Washington Hinter, Senior," said the older guy, then he shook Gabe's hand vigorously.

"My friends call me Gabe, or G-man," said Gabe, taking a big old cup of the strong coffee that was handed to him.

"My friends just call me George, Sr.," said Mr. Hinter.

"Yes sir, Mr. George, Sr.," said Gabe.

There was something special about Mr. Hinter, Gabe could see it in his eyes. It was a good-of-you-to-be-here-look, or something. The old guy's voice had a very cordial ring to it. It was as though he really was pleased with himself and the world. He smiled after everything he said. His big lips curled on the edges into a permanent smile or something, adding to the pleasantness he exuded. He made Gabe feel relaxed at once.

Gabe realized that Bobcat's name was George Washington Hinter, Junior. He must not be proud of that name. He hadn't mentioned his real name at all. Gabe had to just wonder about that one. Bobcat spoke up.

"Dad, Gabe, G-man, Owens, we call him 'G-man,' said he be looking for some work and whatnot. Do you know where he might get a job? Y'all got any openings up at the hospital?" said Bobcat, then he lit back into the huge plate of food before him.

"As a matter of fact we will need a man on our scrubbing crew. A young boy named, Abe Jones, from Fluvanna will be fired. He's got to drinking and don't half come to work. Percy Williams, his supervisor, have to let him go," said Mr. Hinter. "If you want a job Gabe, I can get you one this morning."

"Yeah … I know Abe Jones. Grew up with him. We went to the same schools. We lived in the same neighborhood. I never knew him to drink that much. I know. He must've had some hard and terrible experiences.…

"Yes, I'll take the job. I need a place to stay and all. I just came up here from Fluvanna my own-self. I happened to meet your son up at the bus station yesterday. Good thing, I guess," said Gabe. He lit into the bacon and eggs first, then the pancakes and sausage-links, next. Then Bobcat brought up something that Gabe would've rather he had not.

"Dad, I met this little dude at the bus station yesterday. That stupid Tyrone Smith and his bunch of fags were talking about punking Gabe, here. Ty got raped down at Hanover. He got out of the jail, but can't get the jail out of him. We tried to stomp a mud hole in that sucker," said Bobcat. "Don't nobody want to hear that crap!"

The old guy got up from the table, pulled a pack of Lucky Stripes out of his shirt pocket, flipped one out, mouthed it, and struck a match and lit it. He puffed away on the cigarette. He looked at Bobcat with a little half-smile. "I'm glad you got that red-bone rascal. We don't need his crap in our 'hood–that dope, or the other. They got to keep that stuff to themselves. Each to his own. But he ain't got no right to be raping little boys and whatnot like he and his boys been doing around here," said Mr. Hinter.

"Well, it's about seven-thirty, Gabe. We got to head on up the way. Let me go in the room there and slip out of my house clothes and into my uniform. Be right out," said Mr. Hinter.

"Yes, sir!" said Gabe, glad to get started right, even if he hadn't gotten any sleep at all, was still a little woozy from the beer and booze, and had his first sex hangover from Brenda Crenshaw. Life was still getting better, though.

Mr. Hinter came back into the front room to where Gabe was seated wearing one of those uniforms that he had seen the janitors wearing on the bus. Then Gabe spied Bobcat, heading right on back to one of the doors on a little hallway to a bedroom. *Why ain't this grown dude getting ready to go to work? He been out all day and all night jiving around, now he's going to bed and his dad is going out to work! That doesn't add-up!* Gabe just had to wonder about that one, for real.

Nothing that he had seen so far made any sense to Gabe. How people lived like the people lived that he was seeing on Vinegar Hill was hard to square in Gabe's mind. The sun shown over the horizon like a big old orange basketball. Its reddish-rays filled up the sky with a bright yellow light. Mr. Hinter and Gabe hiked on up Commerce to Sixth Street to Main Street, turned right on Main and headed on up Main towards the University of Virginia Hospital. As Gabe passed the various streets up to Main, he noticed old women with scarves, or handkerchiefs, or just some rags, tied around their heads, wearing baggy dresses, and some were barefoot, coming out on falling-down porches seemingly just to peer at the crowd of marching janitors, maids, cooks, orderlies, nurse's aides, and such menials trudging off to their daily occupations; that was something else, now: *What were they staring at?* he wondered.

When Gabe had walked by Random Row, he felt a little shaky, but it didn't seem quite as scary of a place as it had at night. It was full of broken wine and whiskey bottles, old beer cans and discarded trash. Buildings were crumbling and falling down. Weeds had taken over the street, and what was once shrubbery had become little trees. The place made Gabe think of the word, *Cancer*. It was a cancer that Gabe hoped would not be allowed to spread. *What really happened there?* wondered Gabe.

On Main Street on the way up to the hospital, the scenery changed abruptly as Gabe walked along beside Mr. Hinter. He saw nice, new businesses, housed in the most modern buildings. The Pontiac-Cadillac car dealership was flanked by Trevor Jewelers, where diamonds sparkled reflecting the sunlight, then he saw

Paxie Taxi, Bob Clincher Appliances, Midtown Market, and Seventh Street Drugstore. Farther up Main were The C&O station and railway underpass, only a couple of blocks, or so, from the University Hospital. Then there was a Safeway store, flanked by a Sears and Roebuck store, and a Ben & Franklin five-and-ten-cent store.

As Gabe and Mr. Hinter made their way to Jefferson Park Avenue, the air took on a perfumed fragrance from all of the flowers surrounding the hospital's grounds. Tall Oak trees graced the grounds, as well as shimmering Evergreens, exquisite Pine trees, and some trees Gabe had no idea what type they were. Squirrels played unmolested among them all. Then Gabe saw the five-story hospital.

As they entered the hospital from the Main-floor side, Gabe witnessed the pronounced smell of rubbing alcohol, or something. Multicolored red, white, and blue tiles on the floors shined so bright that the floors looked clean enough to eat off of. The hallways were full of doctors and nurses and well-dressed white professionals.

After Gabe and Mr. Hinter walked up a short hallway, they came to three sets of elevators: One had the word "STAFF," written over it. "GUESTS" was written over another. "SERVICE STAFF," was written on a third. A loud, female's voice blaring over the intercom startled Gabe at first. "Dr. Sperry, Dr. Sperry, Code Twelve on North-Five. Dr. Sperry, Dr. Sperry, Code Twelve on North-Five, please...." *What in the heck is a Code Twelve?* wondered Gabe. Mr. Hinter interrupted Gabe's thoughts.

"Son, no matter what you do, don't forget, you've got to use the service elevators at all times. You will be fired if you don't," said Mr. Hinter. A certain look of knowing showed on the faces of both he and Gabe. "You're never to cross over onto 'their' territory while up here at work on this job. It's unpardonable, un'erstand?"

"Yeah ... I understand," replied Gabe. Deep down within, Gabe pondered the thought, *Why the hell can't we all use any of the elevators? That's so stupid! It's that old segregation crap again! Maybe, dad was right about all of that stuff!* The thought made Gabe very sad. He almost felt like crying.

It peed Gabe off to see two finely dressed Black women also getting on the service elevators. They looked like guests. *The service elevators must be for Black guests also,* thought Gabe. *Now that's a low-down shame. I bet they're paying the same prices, if not more, that the whites are paying, to be treated like the hired-help. That's totally screwed-up!*

They rode the elevator with Gabe and Mr. Hinter to the Subbasement. The doors of the elevator popped-open.

One of the fine-looking women asked Mr. Hinter, "Sir, which way to the 'colored ward?' We're lost!"

"Ma'am, go right, just 'round that hallway, there," he pointed around the back of the service elevators. "Go down that narrow passageway. You will come to a hallway where the lights are dimmed. Follow the black tiles on the floor past the morgue, and you will see a brown door. Go through it. That's where the 'colored ward' is."

"Thank you, sir!" chimed the beautiful ladies.

As they walked away, Gabe followed them for a moment. He soon came to flooring that had no tiles, just cement flooring. Up overhead, he saw a big water pipe in the ceiling, that had to be responsible for a little puddle of water on the floor. Gabe didn't want to see more, so he turned away feeling very disgusted.

When Gabe came back to where Mr. Hinter stood waiting for him to return, Mr. Hinter read the frustration and disgust on his young face. He got a twisted smile on his broad lips.

"Son ... You'll get used to it 'fore long!" said Mr. Hinter with a shrug of his athletic-looking shoulders. He blinked his eyes too, like he was fighting back the tears.

They arrived at a big brown door in the Subbasement with white letters on it, "Housekeeping Department," it said. Mr. Hinter knocked on the door.

"Come in. The door's open," said a voice that sounded somewhat like a whine, but with a sort of cheerfulness. Mr. Hinter opened the door, walked in with Gabe following close behind him. With his hands clasped behind his back, eyes downcast, and his feet shuffling, Mr. Hinter allowed, "Good morning, Mrs. Christian. I hope you're feeling fine this morning. I'm doing all right."

"Well, I'm fair-to-middling, George. Can't complain. Who's that you got there?" asked the gray-haired old lady, wearing a black dress under a starched, white smock. Assistant Director was on a plaque on her big, brown, desk.

"Oh, this-here is Gabriel Owens, Mrs. Christian. He's from Fluvanna. Let me tell you up front, he's a good boy...."

"George, that's all right. You don't have to go on. I'll hire as many of these boys as I can find. I get a bad one–like Abe Jones–now and then, but most of them are good people," said the old lady. She got to blinking her green eyes a little. Her eyes were all made-up like Marilyn Monroe's, or something, seemed like to Gabe.

This lady obviously didn't get to know Abe that well. He's not one of the bad ones, thought Gabe. *Or that wouldn't have come out of her bright-red-lips.*

The old lady reached into her big old brown desk and got out a job application from one of its drawers. She looked Gabe right in the eyes for a moment.

"Sit down over there at that little table over yonder, Gabe. Let's see how well you can read and write. Don't forget to answer all the questions, now," the old lady said, looking at Gabe out of the corner of her left eye.

I bet she thinks I can't read and write, or something, was what Gabe felt. *I'll show her!* Gabe filled out the application so fast that Mrs. Christian looked surprised.

"Son, did you fill-in all the blanks" she asked, examining it very carefully in unbelief, discovering that Gabe had not missed any questions. "You're a smart one," she allowed, a smile went across her rouge and pancake made-up face.

The granny shook her head, an admiring gleam came to her wrinkled face as she got a box of chocolates out of one of the desk's drawers. "Go on, have one Gabe," she said, opening the box to expose an assortment of chocolate-covered nuts.

Gabe took two or three of the Brazil nuts, popped one in his mouth, then smiled. Mr. Hinter just laughed as did Mrs. Christian.

"That's a good boy. Now, you go with Mr. Hinter, he's your supervisor. You'll be working with his scrub crew. Do what he tells you and you can't go wrong. You will be all right, okay Gabe?" said the old lady. Then she lit-up a Parliament filtered cigarette. She got a big UVA cup off the top of one of the four file cabinets in her office, poured herself a cup of coffee out of a big, white, coffeepot she had boiling on a portable hotplate. Her cup was big enough to hold two and a-half regular cups. She took hers black, no cream or sugar. She saluted Gabe and Mr. Hinter with the cup, took a sip and smiled a broad smile, revealing false teeth. "See you boys at lunchtime, now," she said.

Why is she calling Mr. Hinter a 'boy,' he certainly is no boy. I bet he's much closer to her age than he is to mine, thought Gabe.

Gabe and Mr. Hinter went over to the supply room, got buckets, scrubbing-towels, and a gallon jar of Staph-Fine, sanitary cleaner. The cleaner was so strong that you were not to allow it to touch your bared skin. The directions on the jar cautioned against getting it in your eyes and if you have done so, seek immediate medical help. The instructions on that jar made Gabe nervous enough. A phone on the wall of the supply room rang. Mr. Hinter answered it.

"Oh, hello … We'll get right to it," said Mr. Hinter into the phone's reciever. "Gabe come on with me. We got to go scrub a room on North-Five. A patient checked out of that room for good as we were coming in," said Mr. Hinter, a serious look came over his otherwise jolly face.

I think I know what Code Twelve means now. It means that somebody's dying, Gabe figured.

"We have to scrub a room whenever a patient leaves it one way or the other. Or, when a patient has an open infection, we have to scrub that room often too. That's what we'll be doing–you and me, today. We got ten men, but they're all scheduled off today. On Saturdays and Sundays, usually only two of us work. If not for you, I'd be by myself today," said Mr. Hinter, with a hint of sorrow in his mostly cheerful voice.

"Can I rent that spare room Bobcat says you got, Mr. Hinter?" asked Gabe.

"Sure, son. Long as you pay rent and board, you'll always be able to rent that room. Can move right in tonight, even. You can take your meals with us, and I can see that you ain't got no luggage with you, so you can wear the uniforms we will issue you till you get paid. I charge seven-fifty a-week in advance. You ain't got no money, so I'll let you pay me for one week and one week in advance when you get paid. First time will take a lot of your check, but after that, you're good to go," said Mr. Hinter. *In all the confusion, Gabe had left his bag of clothes at the bus station.*

Gabe was glad that he was getting it a little together. He hated the fact though, that he was making so little money, only $0.85 cents per-hour. But life goes on. *White starting-janitors made $1.00 an hour,* Gabe hated this fact most.

In the room, Gabe had to wear protective rubber gloves, a precaution gown, and a surgeon's cap and mask. All of that hospital apparel made him sweat, making the work of scrubbing the walls much harder. Just as soon as he and Mr. Hinter got finished with one room, they were called to do another. Add to the above the fact that they had to change the bulky, heavy, curtains that went around each bed in the rooms. Most rooms had only two, but some had four of these curtains. Doing this over-and-over again on Gabe's first day, "Whew!" It was one of the longest days of his life.

That evening, Gabe sat on the last rung of the stepladder they had used upstairs. He was glad to be back in the Subbasement, hoping the phone wouldn't ring anymore before quitting time. Mr. Hinter sat behind a little faded brown desk looking at the floor, no doubt praying that they had scrubbed the last room for that day. The campus clock clanged three-times, more a loud "dong!" then a "clang!"

"That's it, my-man, it's quitting time, Gabe. Let's hit our time cards. Man, I tell you, I'm 'red-to-go!'" said Mr. Hinter, with a big ear-to-ear smile brightening up his tired-looking face.

A long procession of fellow workers were lined up ahead of Gabe and Mr. Hinter at the time clock located on the wall right beside Mrs. Christian's door. After they had finally hit their cards, Mr. Hinter handed a big old plastic bag full of five uniforms to Gabe, including five black ties. That day, Gabe had worn a white smock. He looked towards the elevators, wanting to get on them in a jiffy. *Got my room and board, clothes and all, and I'm hooked-up,* surmised Gabe, feeling that a lot of his problems was solved. He just knew that things had to get better. He was only fifteen cents shy of what his daddy was making. That had to count for something.

"You ready to go on to the house, Gabe 'G-man!' Owens?" asked Mr. Hinter with a little chuckle. "Come on, then, follow old George."

Gabe followed Mr. Hinter out a backdoor that took them to a loading ramp to some steps that lead to a concrete expanse surrounding the loading dock. They went down some more steps and came out on a sidewalk near the edge of the loading dock. "Gabe, from now on, it's best for you to come and go this way, okay?" said Mr. Hinter, showing the same twisted smile he had that morning when he had to send beautiful Black women to an inferior, "colored ward."

"Yes sir," said Gabe, then he hung his head, thinking, *That old segregation crap, again!*

The smell of garbage permeated the air as Gabe and Mr. Hinter made their way out to Jefferson Park Avenue. It stunk! *Must be the anus-end of the hospital,* thought Gabe.

Sirens blasted and emergency vehicles came roaring by them as Gabe and Mr. Hinter made their way up JPA. The hospital's main entrance reminded Gabe of a Roman, or Greek, Temple that he had seen in his social studies books at school. *What a place this UVA Hospital is,* marveled Gabe. The emergency vehicles went to a little entrance to the right of the main entrance. Big white letters spelled, "E-M-E-R-G-E-N-C-Y E-N-T-R-A-N-C-E," on a red background. Ambulances and rescue squad trucks were unloading injured patients, a long line of them. The scene made Gabe feel sorrow in the pit of his guts.

Across from the hospital, Gabe winced at the housing standing there. Some buildings were about to fall down, standing beside some that were fine as could be. A sign near a street entrance read, "Gospel Hill." A few women chatted away with each other loud enough so that anyone passing could clearly hear them. Two of them sat out on the front porch of a modest-looking house in rocking chairs, laughing and talking away. As Gabe and Mr. Hinter attempted to walk by one spoke out.

"Hi George. How you doing? You reckon Tee's go be to church tomorrow? I got something to tell her?" a shapely lady asked. She had big red-rollers in her long black hair. She wore a beige housecoat and black, fussy, bunny slippers. She had a cigarette dangling from her thin lips. Gabe noticed that she also had a very pretty matured face. Light-brown skin, with gray eyes, and a stacked figure were hers. She had her hands on her hips as she spoke. Her voice was husky, and well, sexy.

"I reckon, Mrs. Haney. I got to work though. I only get one or two Sundays a month off. You un'erstand where I'm coming from?" said Mr. Hinter with a little playful smile on his face. Then, he winked at the woman.

"Yeah, George. I know. You work too hard. You sure don't have time for much fun anymore, huh?" said the lady.

"I'll tell Tee you asked about her, Lulu," said Mr. Hinter, hastily.

"Now, you do that, sugar," said Lulu in a very sultry voice.

Mr. Hinter looked disturbed but Gabe wouldn't dare touch that one with a ten-foot-pole. The two men headed on up to Main without saying a word. Loud shouting and clapping disturbed the evening calm. A group of white students came marching up Main Street carrying picket signs with slogans that said: "We Support Integration! Completely Desegregate, Now!" They chanted, "2-4-6-8, We All Want To Integrate! ..." Traffic was stalled, and several policemen escorted them. A tall, white man, wearing a blue blazer, a red and blue tie over a white shirt, tan slacks and brown penny loafers led the marchers, and the chants. Gabe was amazed.

CHAPTER 7

▼

In the evenings after work, Gabe stayed in his modestly furnished room, with just a twin bed, a little bureau, a small closet and a secretary full of books and papers. The books were about Charlottesville and Albemarle County, and Gabe had never seen a private library, up-close, like that one before. In the drawers of the secretary were files containing notes, some typed and some handwritten. Although some were barely readable, Gabe saw that Vinegar Hill was the primary subject being explored. It was as though someone had gotten started researching and collecting materials for a book, or something, but left without finishing the work.

Gabe was dead tired each day after work, so he spent his evenings reading the books, scouring through the readable notes, getting down with some of the history of how Vinegar Hill got its name and how it turned Black. He would fall asleep sometimes while sitting at the secretary reading.

CHAPTER 8

▼

Gabe wondered, *Why is it that Bobcat never goes to work? Day-after-day, the dude gets up early, stays out late, comes home drunk, and gets in bed. How can he get away with that? ...*

"Gabe, supper's ready," a silky smooth, voice chimed. Gabe put down a manuscript titled, "The Irish Settlers of Charlottesville." He whispered to himself, "I'm going to finish this one right after supper."

Mrs. Orthilia gently knocked on a door not far from her kitchen. It was the one to Gabe's room that was located right after the bathroom's door.

Gabe smelled the aroma coming from the kitchen. He was salivating like a hungry hound. He could smell fried chicken, rolls, candied yams, and pork-and-greens, and probably chocolate cake. Man-o-man! He rushed out to the spacious kitchen to the supper table that had been set fit for a king.

As always, Gabe loved the way Mrs. Hinter smiled. It made him think that this lady was from class. She was not, in Gabe's opinion, from Vinegar Hill. She had high cheekbones, almond eyes, a flat face, and very light skin. These were traits found mostly in the mulatto upper class. The reflection of her voice, as she made pains to pronounce every word just right, made her sound like a member of the Black bourgeoisie, perhaps from Washington, D.C., New York, Chicago, Detroit, and or, maybe, Philadelphia. She was just too pretty, and shapely, and sexy-looking, to be old enough to be Bobcat's mother. She looked too young to be married to old George.

Mrs. Hinter came walking on her pretty toes as usual, wearing black pumps, light-blue silk pants, with a matching top that clung to her five-toot voluptuous body, flattering her in every way without compromising her dignity, none whatsoever. In spite of the respect Gabe knew to show her, he also knew that all of this woman looked good to him. Even the way she had the front room arranged was sexy and exotic. But Gabe wondered, *How the hell does she manage to keep this house and herself looking fine as wine, when she nor her grown son works, and the whole family subsists off of the salary of a janitor working up at the UVA?*

The lady was all that a man could want–but? ...

CHAPTER 9

▼

Early one morning, on a day when Gabe didn't go to work, the sound of a big car's motor awakened him. From his side-window, he could see up the alley to the street. A huge black Cadillac, Coupe De Ville, pulled up in front of the house. A Black brother dressed in all black clothing was obviously the driver of the vehicle. He wore white gloves and had a little weird hat perched on top of his head, that Gabe thought made him look simple, or silly. After the brother had pulled the car to the curb, he jumped out quickly, scampered around to the back-doors of the car, snatching open the left-side door. He then stood by that door seemingly at attention. He reminded Gabe of a "toy soldier."

A well built white man stepped out of the car, dressed to-the-nines, wearing a very expensive-looking dark brown tweed suit. His brown wingtips sparkled in the morning sunlight. He carried a diamond studded cane in one hand, and a black leather briefcase in the other. His head sported a Stetson hat that Gabe had, up until then, only seen pictures of in magazines. His thick dirty-blond mustache neatly trimmed on his upper lip was matched by a thick goatee on his chin. His eyes were serpent-like, icy-colored, and cold-looking. His gait exuded a terrible confidence like the prowl of a lion. He kind of threw the cane in front of him as he walked along. He paused for a second, looking this way and that, then he plodded on up to the front door, shaking his head in disgust just before knocking.

A soft wind gushed from the North, shaking the shrubbery across the street. A dark cloud or two floated aimlessly across the sky, alone and seemingly innocuous. Then Gabe heard a rumble or two of distant thunder. A storm brewing up in the Northeast may just be heading towards the "Ville," but maybe not.

Gabe heard the loud rapping noise the guy's cane made when he beat it against the front door. He wondered, *Is this dude trying to knock the door down, or something? Is this white boy trying to strut his stuff in this 'hood, cause Mr. Hinter ain't home and all? No, that can't be—it's broad daylight outside.*

Then, to Gabe's amazement, Mrs. Hinter all but floated to answer the front door, wearing a fluffy pink housecoat and matching bunny slippers. Her long black hair was still up in big old rollers, and her face was still in night cream, that made it appear to be green, or something. Proud as she usually presented herself, Gabe thought that it was a wonder she had come to her front door looking like, well....

"Mr. DiCappio! Come on in. How good it is to see you. Bring Leroy, if you like. Let me get you all a drink ... or anything you want ..."

"Naw, Tee!" the denizen of organized crime allowed. "I'm not thirsty. I don't want that Roy should see what goes down. It's family business. He might see too much. I like keeping Roy around," said this rough-looking guy, in a thick northern brogue, then his icy-eyes became even more like a shark's.

"Now, cut the crap, Tee. I'm a busy man these days. Got too much business to handle to stand around listening to youse people," said the well dressed anus-hole. He strutted on past Tee into her house with his pointed nose turned up like he smelled something awful. He pranced like a European nobleman. He held his walking cane like ancient kings did their scepters. He held tight to his black, shiny, briefcase.

"Since the family took over the numbers, guys like me have to lay it on the line to come into youse neighborhoods to collect the loot. It's not a good time for white guys to be prancing around in Black people's backyards. It ain't no good at all, Tee," complained the nervous stuffed shirt.

"Let's see the books for last week, huh? Let's get on with it. I want to hit the fraggin' road as soon as possible," said the guy, sharply.

"All right, Tony," said Tee, "I'll be right back with the books. Just hold-tight," she chimed, then bounced over to the master bedroom. She came back carrying a thick, brown, leather-bound ledger and a matching bank deposit pouch. She sat the ledger down in front of Tony, unzipped the pouch, and pulled out a stack of greenbacks. Both of them sat down at the kitchen table.

When Tony saw the stack of dough, his eyes opened wide. "Jeese, Tee! I got to wonder how in the hell do the poor bastards living over in this slum get to come up with this much loot week after week? It's fraggin' unbelievable! Five G's! If I didn't see it with my own eyes, I wouldn't believe it. I just can't understand this. Just looking over your figures, tells me that you're straight. I can see why the boss pushed to takeover this racket. The only thing kicking our nerves is, the government's looking into making the numbers legit. Can you believe it? Well, here, let me give you your cut," said Tony. He started to counting out Tee's take.

"Fifty ... one-hundred ... Fifty ... two-hundred ... Fifty ... three-hundred ... Fifty ... four-hundred ... Fifty ... five-hundred. There, now, youse guys are all straight—not bad for a week's work around here, eh?" said Tony, with a little derisive chuckle. Gabe saw a snarl on his lips that maybe Tee missed.

"I ain't got no time, Tee. Got to be in Washington, D.C., this evening. The family wants me to do a little job over in the Northeast. Be back next week. See if you can top this week. Remember, the boss looks kindly at youse good earners around Christmastime. See' ya, Tee," said the Great White Ape, then he left.

So, that's where Tee gets all of the finer things she got in this house! She's doing the numbers! She's a numbers-writer! She offers poor folk a chance to earn a little tax-free income, provided that they won. The same poor folk who never think about the drain on their pockets, families and neighborhoods that betting on the numbers causes. That crap is crazy! rolled around in Gabe's young mind.

He had been peeping through the crack of the door. He eased the door completely shut. His mind raced back and forth like a rat in a strange labyrinth. What angered Gabe most was, that he knew that the people were giving up their money to a bunch of criminal-pigs that didn't care a rat's ass about them! It caused Gabe to tighten his jaws in anger and disgust until they hurt him.

Tony's big old car headed on up the street. *If my people would put that money in co-opts and whatnot, they could build homes, businesses, schools, and libraries, to help pull themselves up out of this crap-hole of a slum they're forced to live in. But they would rather to just play the numbers,* thought Gabe.

The sky outside suddenly became black as night. The wind rose up, blowing harder and harder until it howled around the corners of the house like an angry animal growls. Lightning flashed across the sky, cutting through the gross darkness like a great white sword. Its frequent flashes stabbed the darkness, assaulting it, momentarily killing it, but it quickly revived. The thunder rolled and exploded like a thousand cannons firing at the same time. The rain poured, coming down by the bucketfuls, washing up in gullies that immediately became huge streams, gushing around the buildings on the Hill, carrying every kind of trash, grit and grime in their waves. *God don't like ugly!* thought Gabe.

Tee's sobbing caught Gabe's attention even more than the strange, magnificent storm. Gabe thought, *I'll go out there in the hall to watch out for Mrs. Hinter, she's so upset. I wish I could go comfort her, but I'd have to reveal that I've been dipping in her business. Wait, she's saying something.*

"Oh God … Oh, Great Creator! … Help me! Please help me! How can I redeem my soul? How will I face The Ancestors? I am descended from African Kings, Queens and Priests. I'm selling my soul and my virtue for this gambling money. I want to stop, but we would fall to the bottom of the heap over here. That's lower than the scum under a black snake's belly…." Tee lamented.

Down in his heart, Gabe could feel her spirit. *I'm young and all, but, it's like my dad says, "it's that old segregation crap!" It done made it so hard for Blacks to honestly make a living, I reckon, until they feel they got to sell their souls to the "demon, Mammon," to have anything worth having. Tee's caught up in that "Mephistophelean Waltz." I bet there are hundreds of Black people like that in Charlottesville, and well over a hundred over here on the Hill.*

The storm raged on. The raindrops beat against the roof of the house sounding like the pounding of ancient African drums. Gabe pondered Tee's plight further. *Tee wants nice things, but she knows she can't have those if she works as a maid, cook, or nurse's aide. Mr. Hinter don't make enough money to afford one African figurine or mask on their coffee table. To retain some part of her dignity, Tee's papered her house with wallpaper depicting scenes from our African homeland. She's trying to redeem herself from the fear of being mediocre.*

The violent rainstorm subsided, but the storms of life raged on.…

On this particular night, Gabe was home as usual in his room reading the manuscripts left behind by Bill Griot. Some had been written by someone calling himself, "Welsh Winston." This person had written a lot about Charlottesville and Albemarle County. Gabe was very interested in a manuscript that dealt with how Vinegar Hill came into being. All Tee and George, Sr., had told Gabe, was that Bill Griot, a schoolteacher, had once rented the room. He passed away, leaving behind all the research that Gabe was raking through. One day, Tee told Gabe, "We just never got around to getting all that stuff together to put out for the garbage men."

"G, G-man. Come on out that darn room, man. It's about time for you to get out of there and have some fun, homes," said Bobcat. "You need to get some fresh air. Get laid. Get your act together. Get down with the Crew, and whatnot. Man, it's about time for you to learn the ropes. Dig?" said Bobcat. He was dressed in tan khakis, white Converse tennis, and a black Banlon shirt. He wore a little black derby cocked to the side on his head. He had a sinister smile on his gangster face.

"Gabe, baby, I want you to hang with me and my main-men, tonight. We're going to get it on tonight. It's getting real dark outside–just right, homes. Get up, get ready, cause here we go, getting ready to do it," said Bobcat.

Not knowing what else to do, Gabe jumped up, put on a pair of tan khakis, a black Banlon shirt, white Converse tennis, and got a newly bought black derby and plopped it on his head just like Bobcat had. He ditty-bopped right on behind Bobcat on out the door into the night air. They were joined by James and Bubbles.

"They played Clemson tonight. I know Virginia's lost! Let me get my transistor radio on ... see who won!" shouted Bobcat. He turned the radio on and tuned-in to WINN Radio:

"We interrupt our regularly scheduled program to bring you the following news. A group of students at UVA's Scott's Stadium gathered on the fifty-yard line tonight, waving signs and placards demanding that the UVA admit more Black athletes. One of their leaders, Stanley Graham Longfellow, a fifth-year Political Science Major, led the chant: '2-4-6-8, We All Want To Integrate!' It took a number of campus and city police almost an hour to escort all of the students off the field. Finally, sanity was restored. The President of the UVA had no comments at this time, except to say, that the matter will be looked into and charges would be pending based upon what infractions various committees discovered, ..." hit Gabe loud and clear.

James looked at Bobcat and Bubbles, then they slapped hands. They all extended their hands to Gabe. He didn't know what else to do, so he gave them some dap. A fifth of Old Crow appeared. Gabe didn't see whose pocket it came out of. The boys got busy throwing her down. Then Gabe took as big of a swig as he could stomach. He still wasn't one of the boys yet, when it came to guzzling liquor. But he tried. The booze went to his head immediately. Made him woozy, then high.

The quartet bopped on up Preston Avenue. The lights got dimmer as they trudged on over to Rugby Road. The houses got finer and finer, were all bricked up, and some resembled mansions. *What the hell are we going up here for? This is the white-folk's part of town. Have Bobcat and them forgot what it is?* Gabe wondered.

Bobcat held up his right hand, signaling for the Crew to stop. He whispered, "Get down. Get down behind those hedges, y'all."

Gabe heard the gong-gong! ... sound of the University's clock go-off ten-times. *I wonder why Bobcat got us all hiding and whatnot?* thought Gabe.

A cool breeze drifted through the hedges, bringing with it a heavy perfumed fragrance from a multiplicity of summer flowers growing in the yards of Rugby Road residents. Up until then, the night was quiet except for that little breeze. The fraternities blasting music at parties going on several blocks away, could barely be heard. Gabe got warm and uncomfortable hiding behind those hedges and was minded to get up from there. A foreboding feeling made him even more restless.

A drunk person came stumbling down the sidewalk, walking like a child attempting to take its first steps. He wore a blue Blazer, tan slacks, a light-blue shirt, with a red-and-blue-striped tie, and brown penny-loafers. He sort of staggered to and fro, making only a little forward progress at a time. He was not only drunk, but lost as well. He certainly was headed in the wrong direction.

The moonlight cast a hazy, shadowy pattern on the sidewalk making the night seem like a page out of the "twilight zone." Bobcat's lips twisted up into a mean frown as his face became one huge snarl. The muscles of his jaws started jumping, pulsating, and trembling. His nose flared and his eyes narrowed, the closer the drunk student got to the hedge where the quartet hid. Bobcat eyed the student with nothing but cold contempt.

"You nasty, rich, sucker," whipped out of the side of Bobcat's ashen-lips. "Up-you! And up-your momma, too! You're rich cause of what you all did to my people. I'd be a Prince today if your people would've left my people in they homeland, Africa! Now, you want us to be your 'Niggers!' I got your 'Nigger!' swinging, sucker," yelled Bobcat.

Gabe shuddered when he saw where this mess was going. He stayed put when Bobcat, James and Bubbles leapt from behind the hedge all at once and grabbed at the student. Bobcat reminded Gabe of a big old cat pouncing on a mouse.

The blond-headed student with buckteeth and freckles on his face tried to run but stumbled and fell. He got up to try to run again. A lick caught him square on the back of his head, thrown by Bobcat, with his eyes shining like the moonlight.

"I'm a militant mo-joe!" screamed Bobcat. He slammed one of his massive fists into the back of the student's head again. The student rolled over on the grass right beside the sidewalk. His breathing became just convulsive attempts. *That guy looks familiar. Is he-he-he still alive! He looks glassy-eyed. His tongue done come out, hanging way out of his mouth. Blood is oozing out of his mouth, nose, and one ear. Oh, my ...* screamed inside of Gabe's head. He ran from behind the hedge.

The contents of Gabe's stomach came gushing up his throat and out of his mouth. A cold, icy, feeling engulfed his very being. His hands trembled like tree leaves blowing in a hot summer's wind. Suddenly the moonlight turned into a greenish haze. The hedges became shadows of death. The stench of death filled the air.

Oh my God, what am I doing out here with these … What am I going to do! I know that student's dead! I got to get away. I got to get … I got to watch it—they will kill me too! Better not run right now … Ah … that boy is dead as hell! Wish I had stayed home. Mean as my daddy was, he never did kill nobody! thought Gabe, with his stomach twisting up into painful knots.

Bubbles ran to the corpse. He tore an expensive-looking class ring off the guy's finger. It had rubies or something set in white gold. James pulled off the guy's expensive-looking penny-loafers. He actually smiled at the dead student, like Satan does at a lost soul. Bobcat went through the dead guy's pockets. His wallet was full of big bills: tens, twenties, fifties, and hundreds, stacked in there.

"Hey, dudes! Listen up! We got the doggone money. Let's blow this scene!" shouted Bobcat. "We got to split!"

Confusion and psychological distress caused Gabe to dive back behind the hedges. His sobbing made his stomach ache, and caused a throbbing pain in his head.

In a few minutes, Bobcat's wallop up beside Gabe's head brought him back to reality. "G-man, what the hell are you lagging behind for? Do you want to get picked up by the cops behind this caper, dude? Huh? Huh? What the hell is the matter with you, anyway? Don't you hate those white mo-joe's just as bad as we do? Well, you'll learn to hate them as time goes on. Wait till you hear what they did … Well, let's just get the hell out of here right now, G," shouted Bobcat. "We ain't got no time to rap, okay?"

Like in a dream, Gabe ran behind the walk-partners like a zombie. The indelible image of the dead student stamped itself on Gabe's mind: *The white dude's mouth hung open like a slaughtered hog. His blood stained the grass, the sidewalk, my life. I will never be able to forget this night. I'm going to see that lump on the head of that guy in my mind forever. I feel like puking up.* Gabe started to dry-heave. He couldn't get anything up.

Soon they arrived on the edge of Vinegar Hill on Preston Avenue. Tears eased down Gabe's cheeks. He trembled all over. He realized that, *I'm among cold-blooded killers!*

What shocked Gabe the most was Bobcat, James and Bubbles, slapping hands, laughing and cutting up like they had just come back from a boy scout excursion. They had just murdered another human being. Gabe wanted to see at least a little remorse. But no! …

"All right, listen up!" shouted Bobcat. "Let me count this loot, see how much each walk-partner gets."

He pulled the student's wallet out of his khakis. It was shiny, brown, polished leather. Bobcat got out the stack of dollar bills. Gabe knew that this was blood-money. He dry-heaved again.

"G-man, what the hell is the matter with you! Huh!" screamed Bobcat, with his lips pulled up, showing dirty-white teeth, making him resemble an angry wolf.

"G, you're starting to act like a pussy-boy. Was Ty right about you? Now we came to your aid cause we thought you were going to be a tight-brother. Now, how are you going to act?" yelled Bobcat, further excoriating Gabe, staring him right in his eyes, so close to Gabe's face, he could smell his foul breath. Bobcat's eyes burnt right through Gabe.

"What's it going to be, G-man? Are you a righteous dude, or a pussy-boy?" asked Bobcat, with James and Bubbles flanking him like they had the first time Gabe had met them. The moment conjured up deep psychological reverses in Gabe's mind: *"Shut up that crying, boy! ... Don't you make another sound ... You hear me! Now, you do what the hell I tell you to do—got that?"* These orders were programmed within Gabe so emphatically from Allen his father that they invaded his conscious mind automatically when he heard the demon in his father speaking out of Bobcat's mouth. He snuffed up all of his outward protestations, put on a thin, quirky smile, then he pretended to go along with "his walk-partners." Inwardly his emotions boiled like a volcano. He formed a silly grin on his twisted, trembling lips.

"Look, G-man, we got over a thousand dollars, here. I figure we're all in it for about two-hundred-fifty apiece. That's what your cut is, dude," said Bobcat. When Gabe vehemently shook his head, Bobcat's eyes bucked out in anger.

"No! ... No! I don't want any!" shouted Gabe in protest. "Bobcat, you can help yourself to my share. That's all right. I didn't do enough to get a share," shouted Gabe, wanting nothing to do with the blood-money that made him want to puke every time he thought about that dead student.

Bobcat, James and Bubbles rushed over to surround Gabe. Bobcat yelled right in his face. "G, come here to me, punk." Then he grabbed the shoulders of Gabe's shirt. "I believe you're trying to screw with me, my-man. I ain't no humping-chump, dude. Do you think I'm a fool or something?" shouted Bobcat, standing so that he was eye-to-eye with Gabe. He could feel Bobcat's hot breath on his face. That look in Bobcat's eyes was another murder getting ready to happen, or something. Gabe didn't want the next victim to be him. James and Bubbles stood waiting for the lead-dog to take the first bite. Gabe started to whimper out of fear. Bobcat turned him loose. He drew back his right fist, but decided not to bring it down on Gabe.

"Here, chump. Take this money and get the hell out of my face. You ain't no down-brother. And I better not hear a fraggin' word about what happen tonight. We live in the same house. I'll slit your throat, you coward. Pick up that darn money. You heard me–pick it up, sucker!" shouted Bobcat. James shoved Gabe in the direction of the money lying on the ground. Bubbles forced him to bend over. Again Gabe heard the demon that was in his father: *"Do what I tell you to do, boy! Or I'll! ..."*

To obey was the only way to safety. So he scooped up the blood-money, made a little bundle of it, and stuffed it into his front pocket. The UVA clock "gonged!" three-times. The "walk-partners" went their way. Left Gabe alone. He dashed along Preston to Fourth Street. He stumbled and fell down once or twice. He cried like a whipped child. *How in the hell did I get into all of this crap? What did I do to make God punish me like this? I ain't never hurt nobody! I ain't never seen nobody killed before! Oh God, how will I ever get over this?* flooded Gabe's mind as he ran up Fourth Street as fast as he could.

Gabe scampered home that early morning gasping for breath. He wondered: *How will I ever get over this crap? I can see that guy's face right now! Bobcat and them are stupid fools. All white folk ain't bad. What am I going to do with this money? It's haunted with the innocent blood of that student. Bobcat had no right to take out his hatred on an innocent person, just like white folk ain't got no right to attack and kill innocent Black folk!* He dropped the money on the sidewalk.

Gabe just got into bed. He couldn't sleep. He was glad when daylight rolled back the darkness. He figured he'd start to move by inches towards forgetting.

CHAPTER 10

▼

On this Friday evening, Bobcat pranced through the house wearing gray dress slacks, a blue Van Hussein shirt, spit-shined penny-loafers, a red and black tie, with his same old black derby perched on top of his head. Gabe could see his face in the shine on those penney-loafers. He guessed it must've took all that scrubbing and cleaning to get the blood off them. Gabe watched him from a corner of the hallway.

"Come on G-man. I know you're there. You should be over the caper by now. It's a little hard the first time, but life goes on, dude. We all been there. You're acting like an old sissy-bookworm. Come on let's go on out and have some fun. The homies want us to go with them down to the Odd Fellows Hall. We're going to get our dance on tonight, homes," said Bobcat with a boyish chuckle.

Gabe came into the front room from the little hallway behind the kitchen. "I got to go to work tomorrow. I'm a be on with just your father. The rest of the scrubbing crew is off," said Gabe in a shy and coy way. His voice vibrated from the fear of Bobcat that he felt down within himself. What Gabe was feeling was, *Every time that guy goes anywhere, he ends up in some violent crap with somebody. He always got to prove that he's the man—the mightiest of them all. I know he's going to start some mess at the Hall. But I got to go with him.*

"I got to get my rags tight. I'll be out, okay?" said Gabe, his voice barely rising to a whisper.

Them Odd Fellow Hall dances always turn into brawls. Somebody got to get messed up. I don't know why my people can't just come to the dance hall, have fun, leave peacefully, and that be the end of it. Why a fight has to happen is beyond me. But here we go again. Hope I'm wrong tonight, reverberated in Gabe's mind.

Gabe got on his black dress suit, a white shirt, a blue and white striped tie, plain black shoes, that were not even polished, let alone, spit-shined. He would have rather not gone to the Hall, anyway. He walked into the front room and took a swig out of a pint of Old Crow Bobcat offered him. The liquor went down a lot easier now that he'd gotten used to guzzling it.

"Bobcat, who's playing down the Hall tonight?" asked Gabe.

"Little Clay and the Joy Rockers. Go be a stone throw-down. They got a groovy sound, man. I hope you're digging what I'm saying," said Bobcat.

Gabe took a couple more hits of the booze. The night became all fuzzy and whatnot. "Let's go, Bobcat, I'm ready to go bogey," said Gabe.

At about ten-thirty, Bubbles, James and Bobcat, with Gabe trudging along, made the scene at The Odd Fellows Hall on East Market Street, that Preston Avenue ran into. The place was full to capacity as usual. The rectangular dance floor was very large, some 45-50 x 55-60 feet, or so. But with all of the mix of people from all over Charlottesville, and Albemarle County, and surrounding counties, such as Fluvanna, Greene, Madison, Orange, and Augusta, the dance floor seemed variously crowded. Huge Crowds always made Gabe feel uncomfortable.

All of the dudes and girls were decked in their best, clean as could be, man. Such fine clothes they wore: two-piece suits, jazzy miniskirts, some sporting Stetson hats, bright-red ties, shiny new shoes, spit-shined, and whatnot. Like sardines in a can, they stood around the place, with its aging moldings in the ceiling, and rough painted walls all around, and that out-of-date decor on the stage, and rough hardwood floors. The people slipped flasks of liquor out of their ladies' bags, and coat and pants pockets. They jived around waiting for the band to get on the stage and get going.

Then the band members sauntered out on the stage coming out of a side-door. Dressed in red and blue tuxedos, and black patten leather shoes, they made Gabe think of the term "sugar-sharp," as an adequate description of them. The drummer sat down behind an enormous set of drums, with the red and white logo, "*Joy Rockers,*" emblazoned in red on an orange crest on the face of the bass drum. The drums were also red and blue. The drummer started a drum roll on his snare drum. The rest of the band marched to their instruments mounted near the front of the stage. They picked up a trumpet, saxophone, trombone, a lead guitar, a bass guitar, and one of them pranced over to an electric piano. The band got to popping out "Cleo's Back!" Their conked hair bounced up and down but always came back into place. They were all deep-ebony with bright smiles resembling the keys on a piano. The music got the people to dancing, right away.

Three singers came dancing onto the stage. Two were very light-skinned men. A girl among them could've passed for white. Even had blond-ish hair and light-green eyes. But her lips gave her away. The men had on the same attire as the rest of the band members. The girl had on a micro miniskirt. Gabe thought she was so hot. They belted out the "Marking Bird," song. Gabe loved that song.

He got to dancing his own way, doing the twist with a country high-step or two mixed in. The city girls just loved that. They started to cut-in to get their chance to dance with the cute country boy. Then, Gabe heard the commotion.

"Monkey-jumper, I done told you … I'm going to get you back! You and your boys jumped me up at the bus station the other day. My main-men wasn't with me. Now, it's payback time, suckers!" Ty Smith screamed. Gabe heard him even over the loud music.

"Come on, then. Come on get some!" yelled Bobcat right back at Ty. "Yeah, now you're right, sucker!"

Ty pulled out a long knife and clicked it open. Women started screaming all around Gabe. People jammed the doorway. For a while, nobody could get out. Then they burst out the doors like a herd of animals headed into a slaughter pen. Ty must've blanked. Bobcat hit him all of a sudden. The knife went through the air. Ty went down to the floor. Again, his boys hit the door, leaving Ty behind. James, Bubbles and Bobcat took turns stomping Ty in front of all the people. They got to spinning him around with each blow. Ty groaned and then broke down and cried. *I feel so sorry for Ty, man. Nobody deserves to be brutalized and humiliated like that. Bobcat and them need to leave the man a little thread of dignity,* thought Gabe.

The blood running out of Ty's nose reminded Gabe of the dead student. Ty stumbled up off the floor, his eyes were swollen, and his face a mass of knots, cuts and bruises. He wobbled to and fro for a minute or two. When he tried to rub the left side of his face, the pain that caused made him withdraw his hand very quickly. Some of the cuts were deep lacerations.

"I'm going to get your cock-strong ass, Bobcat! You and them fags you be walking with. I'm going to get all y'all if it's the last thing I do! I'm going to kill you, Bobcat!" screamed Ty, then he ran out of the Hall into the night.

"Yeah, come on back, sucker. I got your 'I'm going to kill you Bobcat!' swinging. Come on back. Let's see who end up getting killed," replied Bobcat.

"Right-on!" shouted James and Bubbles. Gabe felt sick to his stomach.

Bobcat, James and Bubbles left the Hall right after the fight. Gabe had had enough. *I ain't never going to follow them crazy guys around again. I don't want nobody else thinking I'm one of them. I ain't never going to kill nobody cause they're white or rich. I got to get the murder of that white boy they killed off my conscience. I can't live with that crap on my mind any longer. Somehow, I got to go to the cops. That's the only way to get this stuff off my chest, off my mind, and out of my conscience,* was the way Gabe figured he had to go.

As Gabe was leaving the Hall, he eyed a tall, heavyset white cop with "Bill Mawyers" on his name tag. He had a lot of hash marks on his sleeves, and sergeant's patches on the arms of his jacket. He and two other lower-ranked white police officers had to have stood idly by and watched Bobcat and them fight. They hadn't lifted a finger. Gabe wondered, *How in the hell can they call themselves security? Had they stepped outside while the fight went on? Didn't they hear the commotion? I know: "Let the Niggers go ahead and kill one another," was probably what they felt. By law, the Hall had to provide security, but the security didn't have to care about the Blacks at the dances. The off-duty white police officers certainly weren't going to lookout for the safety of people they despised—if they could help it.*

As Gabe walked the short distance to where he rented, he rehearsed in his mind what he'd seen of Charlottesville—the Ville—thus far: *In a few months, I've seen poor Black men, downtrodden and scared, taking their spite out on each other, a University student, and poor Black women. The more I see, the worse it gets. I expect to see hell erupt up on the Negroes on Vinegar Hill. I know it will happen, and spillover onto the rest of Black Charlottesville. It's something that has to happen. Things couldn't be worst. There's nowhere else for things to go. "I know a change go come!"*

PART II

CHAPTER 11

▼

Gabe lingered at the breakfast table after George, Sr., had long finished eating, pushed back his chair, left the kitchen area, and was getting ready to go to work. His appetite was not all that great these days. A radio news flash came at the end of the horrible noise some English rock group had been making–that stuff all sounded the same to Gabe. He grooved on the music and songs of James Brown, or Joe Tex, Otis Redding, and or, Diana Ross and the Supremes.

"Still no leads to who was responsible for the gruesome murder of Stanley Graham Longfellow, a UVA civil rights activists, and honors graduate student …" went the WINN news break. "This is Brad Blueberry, and I will be back with the latest news after a word from our sponsors…."

His stomach knotted right up, and Gabe stood up from the table right away. It suddenly clicked in Gabe's mind where he'd seen that murdered student before: *That guy was the leader of that group of radical whites opting for the recruitment of more Blacks for the UVA, I saw that first evening after I'd started working. Oh, God, man! That's who Bobcat and them killed! One of the few friends we got up there on that racist campus. Those stupid! … I got to tell somebody in law enforcement all about what I know,* puffed up in Gabe's mind causing terrible pain in his temples. The news went on, "There have been several brutal attacks on male students on Rugby Road, lately. Most occur near Fraternity Row on the upper end of the Street closest to the UVA campus. The campus police and Charlottesville Police homicide investigators say they have no concrete leads, yet; but Lieutenant Clem Doll, a homicide detective with the city, says, 'I believe the assailants may be from the Vinegar Hill area.…'"

Every bit of the news all but choked Gabe. He was scared, thinking, *Them cops are getting too close to us—them! Man, I got to free myself from this mess. Can't sleep. Can't eat. I wish I hadn't gone with them that night. I know I failed the test. I can't be no walk-partner, if it means beating people to death cause they're a different color than us! How is that different from the Ku Klux Klan?*

Gabe's heart picked up to a faster beat when he heard the rest of the news. "Although, city police have no real leads in the case at this time, Chief of Police, Captain Lennie Moon, states, 'Now … For my money, I'm pretty sure that most of the attacks on our fine students up at the UVA, including this latest murder, is the work of a few Black thugs who reside in that God-awful slum, Vinegar Hill. I strongly believe that as long as it exists in our fair city, brutal assaults, rapes and murders will continue. To get rid of those crimes, we have to first get rid of that slum, and all other Black slums, too.'"

Gabe felt as though Chief Moon and Lieutenant Doll were looking right through that radio at him. George, Sr., flicked the radio off. His usual quiet face got wrinkled in a very deep frown. His eyes started to tremble.

"Them nasty crackers are all the time blaming us folk down here for every dead-blame bad thing that happens up at that school. Why it always got to be us?" hissed out of George, Sr.'s lips. The tension in the air thickened like the humidity does in July.

"I don't know, Mr. Hinter," said Gabe, looking down at the floor like a child caught stealing from a cookie jar. He had to squint his eyes almost shut to conceal the fear in his heart.

"Man, Gabe, I don't want to hear that crap!" said George, Sr.

"Yes sir," replied Gabe, in a whisper.

"Let's go to work," said George, Sr., emphatically.

On up the way to work that morning, Gabe did not utter a word. His conscience weighed him down like a ton of bricks on his head. What turned around in his young mind was, *Sure as shooting, I've got to drop-a-dime on Bobcat and them. Can't deal with this crock of do-do any longer. It's too heavy, man. Got to get it off my back, and whatnot. Just got to! Mrs. Tee and George, Sr., they been very good to me, though.* Gabe rammed his hands into his front pockets, casting his eyes to the sidewalk, a lone teardrop formed in the corner of his left eye.

He hated what he felt he had to do. *I feel like a betrayer, a Benedict Arnold, an old Uncle Tom, or somebody. But innocent blood is innocent blood! And, "Abel's Blood Cries From The Dust! …" I'm so sorry I heard that boy's name. Now, I can't forget the fact that he had family, friends, and associates, and was a fellow-struggler for Black Civil Rights! He was not just a nameless, white face. I've got to do right by him and those who raised him, and his friends and associates. I just hate doing this to old George and Mrs. Tee, though.*

Gabriel ran up ahead of George, Sr. He couldn't stand to look at him any longer. He wanted to get to work before old George, make the phone call, and get it over with. He remembered that a pay phone was up on the wall on North-Five. He dashed up the stairway, running all the way up five flights of steps. His heart beat faster and faster, more from the excitement of the moment than from the run up the stairs. He reflected for a second on the fact that it was cloudy outside that morning, like a storm might bust forth any moment. Now, Gabe knew, a storm of sorts was surely going to come to town.

The newsman on the radio had given the number for the city police station. Gabe dropped a dime in the phone, dialed 555-1313, and the phone rang. He had the receiver to his ear. His body trembled so bad he had a hard time holding on to the receiver. He had to hold on to it with both hands. He listened to it ring for what seemed like an eternity, but was only a little over a minute. Finally, someone picked up on the other end.

"Hello. This is the Charlottesville Police Department. How may I help you?" said a squeaky, female's voice.

Gabe slammed the receiver back into its place. He'd lost his nerve. *I've got to do it!–got! to!–got to!* He just knew that he had to do this.

He dialed the number again. Same response. Only this time, Gabe whined, "I saw three mens beat a student to death on Rugby Road one night. They're, Bobcat, James and Bubbles from over on Vinegar Hill," he blurted out. He took the heavy receiver from his ear. A terrible disgusting feeling engulfed him. He paused for a second or two.

"Please stay on the line, sir … Please, sir, don't hangup … Sir … Sir … what is your name?" the squeaky voice pleaded with Gabe.

Gabe plunked the phone down like it was a ball of fire. *Got to get down stairs before old George comes in and misses me,* he knew the drill.

The crowd of janitors and maids in-line ready to punch in suddenly seemed like cattle waiting at the slaughter pen to Gabe. The nerves of his stomach started to turn over. His guts bubbled, round-and-round. It came down on him all at once. Gabe ran to the Black employee's locker room. He found one of the many stools along the wall in there, and the dung nearly ran out of him like a train does down the tracks.

"Oh God, help me. Help me Lord. Forgive me for any part I played in the killing of that innocent student. Forgive me for not doing everything possible to stop Bobcat and them. I may never feel free from that! God … I'm sorry. Forgive me," prayed Gabe. Big teardrops ran down his dusty cheeks. Then a voice startled him.

"Gabe, I know what's wrong with you. You stay in that darn room at the house too much. A man got to have an outlet. You need to go amongst the ladies more often. It ain't healthy for a young man like yourself to stay up in his room like you're doing," said old George.

"And, Gabe, take something for that diarrhea, son. It stinks," said old George, then he turned up his nose and walked away, laughing to beat the band. Gabe didn't think he was all that funny. *If he knew why I was so upset, he'd not be laughing at all. Probably would be crying instead,* thought Gabe. *I'm going to have to skip town—that's all to it. They will eventually know that I was the cheese-eating snitch. Who else could it have been? I know a walk-partner ain't suppose to rat another one out. Anyone of them will take me out without thinking about it. I'm deep in the do-do, now! I got to play it cool until I figure out a way to blow this town for good.*

CHAPTER 12

▼

"Get up, Gabe. You're off today. I want you to go with me. I promise you, we ain't going to kill nobody. Swear and hope to die," said Bobcat.

I don't want to go nowhere with this ... But I know I had better! Gabe knew deep in his troubled heart that Bobcat had the power over him right then.

"Okay, Bobcat. Let me get up and whatnot. Gabe pulled on his clothes, washed his face, and was ready to hit the streets with one of the guys he now despised more than anyone else in the world. They went down Fourth Street, turned on Commerce and bopped on down to the block. On a corner near Random Row, an old man wearing ragged clothes reached out his hand to Bobcat."Hey, young homes. Let me hold a couple dollars till I get my act together, okay?" the old guy whined like the whinnying of a horse. "I'm a little short."

To Gabe's surprise, Bobcat stopped. His eyes grew sad and glassy. He looked at Gabe for a second, then he rubbed his rock-jaws with a huge hand.

"Hey, Bobby, I know you've been messed up from the War. Uncle Sam didn't give a crap about you Black veterans. You b'long in a hospital–needed that for years. You got to be shell-shocked and whatnot. Here, take this ten-spot," said Bobcat, now seeming to be near tears. He reached into his front pocket with his right hand, got out a ten-dollar bill, gave it right to the old dude. That shocked the hell out of Gabe.

The old wino's heavy glance changed but little. Gabe figured that his mind was no doubt addled from years of being doused with cheap wine and liquor. He probably didn't care nothing about bathing–judging from the way he smelled– proper diet, or nothing else. Like so many others hanging around Random Row, bedding down in those old abandoned buildings, all that mattered to him was getting the next bottle of rotgut. There was a bunch of them on old Random Row.

"I know'd that you's a good one. All the peoples on the Hill they looks up to you and your boys," said the whiny old dude. He took the ten and lifted it up with trembling hands, kissed it, and got a lot more energy getting out of there than he at first seemed capable of. Gabe marveled at the old drunk. He also found it strange, that the dude never said "Thank you." But Bobcat didn't seem to mind. He got a little smug grin on his otherwise hateful looking face, and said, "Let's go."

It's almost like I'm meant to follow this gorilla around. I hate going with him, he got to know that. Yet, he orders me to follow him. I don't want people, like Ty, to think that I'm real close to Bobcat and them anymore. That'll put my life in danger. I can't run. I can't get away. Everybody will know, when they arrest Bobcat and them, that I was the snitch. So, I got to play it cool for a little while longer, thought Gabe. He and Bobcat bopped on down Third Street, the last unpaved, dusty and narrow street before you get to the downtown area. On the corner of Third and Second Streets, James' hovel stood right next to Bubbles'. They lived in two stuccoed shotgun shacks with outdoor toilets, and no indoor plumbing, just like Mary Lou's house. When Bobcat approached Bubbles' house, the one with a little rickety balcony up top, Bubbles was braving that balcony.

"Bubbles. Hey, Bubbles. Get down here, homes. Got some heavy rap to lay on you," said Bobcat.

Bubbles went back inside, came down the stairs and on out the door of his house. "What's happening, Cat?" said Bubbles.

"Don't know it," said Bobcat. He and Bubbles slapped hands. They left Gabe hanging. *Ah, shoot,* thought Gabe.

"I'll see y'all later on the Hill," said Gabe. He went on towards the pool hall. He knew Bobcat would end up there. That's where he always ended up.

Soon as Gabe was out of earshot of Bobcat and Bubbles, Bubbles allowed, "Cat, what you doing walking with that little punk for, man? He acts just like a scared pussy-boy. He ain't no sure'nough walk-partner, man," said Bubbles. "The dude just ain't no hard-down, militant, mo-joe like us. We got to cut him loose."

"Yeah. I know, Bubbles. Remember that old saying, 'keep your friends close and your enemies closer,' that's what we got to do, dig?" said Bobcat out of the side of his mouth. Bubbles dug where he was coming from.

"Cat, we got to get one of our righteous, new walk-partners to off Gabe, that little jive-phony. Homes, he done seen too much to not be in all the way with the Crew. But, dude, he ain't got the heart for it–no killer instinct," said Bubbles.

"I got you, Bubbles," said Bobcat. He slapped hands vigorously with Bubbles.

"Got to get on down to the pool hall, Bubbles, see what's happening, man," said Bobcat. He walked away from Bubbles and headed down by James' house.

"Hey, James. Look here, my-man. Glad you're up. Want to rap to you."

"Okay, Bobcat," shouted James. He came on out of his front door.

"Homes, I done heard the news," whispered James, in a shaky voice.

"What's happening, James?" replied Bobcat. "You all right?"

"The cops been on the radio. They say they b'lieves somebody from over here killed that UVA student ..." croaked James, his voice sounding almost like a frog's.

"James ... James. You starting to act like Gabe, or somebody. What the heck is wrong, homes? That wasn't our first–and it won't be our last," said Bobcat with a bit of harshness ringing in his voice. Bobcat's glance turned from mildly angry to vicious-looking. He balled up his left fist as he spoke.

"Look, James. You got to pull yourself together. Man, you're coming off like a scared faggot. What's happening?" shot Bobcat at James. "Those stupid cops always blaming everything that happens on us Hill-Cats. You know that. You're scared of nothing, man. What's happening? The only link they could have is Gabe. We're going to get rid of that one–believe me!"

"Yeah, but ... Bobcat!"

"Yeah, what, James? Are you finking out on us, now, too?"

"Okay, Cat–you know I'm all in, homes," said James, standing in the street visibly shaking. "Cat we got to cool our game for a few days, though, man," said James in a whine.

"I ain't cooling nothing down, James. If you're with me, you ain't either," shot Bobcat back at James. He was staring at James eye-to-eye.

"Yeah ... Yeah ... I'm down," said James, sheepishly.

"Let me go on over to the pool hall where the real mens are," said Bobcat, refusing to slap hands with James. He left his main-man hanging.

CHAPTER 13

▼

At the pool hall, Bobcat hollered at a former walk-partner gone straight. He owned the hall, a barbershop, and a grocery store. They were all in one large building combined.

"Hey, Jake. What's going on, dude? I been over on the other side of the store, homes, and I ain't never seen so many people in this place at one time. They about to jam you, Jake. What's going on?" said Bobcat.

Jake, a rotund fellow standing at about five-foot, three-inches, wearing a clean cook's apron over black trousers, a white silk-shirt, a tiny black bow tie, and brown wingtip shoes, shined to perfection, answered Bobcat in hushed tones. His cream-and-coffee complexion was covered by only a thin little mustache on his top lip, and the reddish-brown hair on his head. He curled up his thick lips into a smile.

"Cat, man, there's a country-looking, red-bone over yonder at my fifth table–the best table in the hall–who can't shoot worth a dime. But he's losing a bundle on the dudes, shooting dollars, man. Don't make no sense. The Cat's got a big bankroll in his pocket, homes. The homies are over there picking up on some of that. It looks like it's as easy as taking candy from a baby. That's got to be what you're looking for, Cat, dig?" said Jake Taylor.

"Yeah, Jake, baby, I dig," said Bobcat. He winked at Jake. A sneaky smile came on his lips like the look on a fox when it's getting ready to raid the hen-house. He bopped on over to the pool hall from out of the grocery area.

"Good luck, Cat," whispered Jake. He turned his attention to some ladies waiting in the line to be checked out.

"I don't need no luck, Jake. I got skills, homes," replied Bobcat.

Over in the pool hall, the ceiling was up high, but not tall enough to accommodate all of the cigarette and cigar smoke the dudes in the packed place puffed up. Gabe stood over near the entrance by an emergency exit, just in case Bobcat got some crap started again.

Bobcat sized up the dude giving away his money like a chump. He saw a red-bone dude, face the color of Albemarle clay, all fat and awkward-looking, wearing green overalls–like Mr. Green Jeans–big old tan brogan shoes, and a red and blue plaid shirt. The guy must've come up out of Cismont, North Garden, Fluvanna or Louisa, or somewhere like that. And, he had to be the biggest sucker in the world. A lean looking dude watched as the red-bone dude sank a shot in the corner pocket. It was an easy shot–straight in. Any little old lady might've been able to make it.

"Game!" yelled Bobcat. All moved away, knowing better than to get in Bobcat's way. James and Bubbles had made their way to the pool hall, as well as a lot of other members of the Crew, Gabe didn't know by name. He knew them by the way they dressed. Some were already in games on the other tables.

"Right-on," said the red-bone. "You're on."

Bobcat figured that he would be a little generous so that he'd be a greater hero to the Crew. "Look, brother man. I don't want you to drop all your money too soon. It wouldn't look good on my part. The dudes will think I got over on you– no-fair. I want you to feel like I gave you the best shot when we's through, dig?" said Bobcat with a huge smirk on his muscular face.

Okay, homes," said the red-bone, in an exaggerated country drawl. "Let's shoot for ten-dollars-a-game, though, so's it'll be mo' inter'res'ing. Is that all right with you, sir?"

"Hey–that's fine with me. I got a pool stick and chalk, man. Let's get it on," hissed Bobcat, like a cat getting ready to pounce on a mouse.

Jake finished checking out the customers that had waited patiently in one of his two checkout lines. He couldn't wait to see how Bobcat would do against the country guy who was trying to be a pool-shooter. Jake came into the hall just before Bobcat and his boy got the game on.

"Rack'em up, Jake," said Bobcat, giving Jake a little wink.

"Right-on, my-man," said Jake. "What y'all playing, fellows?" asked Jake looking at one then the other.

"Nine-Ball," said Bobcat.

"That'll be all right with me," said the red-bone, with a little sigh. "By the way, I'm called, Big-Red, or just Red."

Bobcat went around the table, grabbed Big-Red's hand and shook it briskly and allowed, "I'm known as Bobcat, the shooting-est mo-joe on this Hill!"

"I'm right pleased to meet you Mr. Bobcat," said Big-Red, laughing shyly.

"Go-head-on, break'em, Red," shouted Bobcat.

Big-Red smiled, got into position on the edge of the pool table, stroked his stick a couple of times, and slammed it against the cue. It took off and crashed into the balls on the table, that scattered all over the table top. To Bobcat's amazement, Red ran all the other balls off the table right quick, making some impossible shots. The Nine-Ball had hugged the rag close to the right side pocket. Red called the shot.

"Corner pocket, straight on up," he said with a dopey-daze on his face.

"I'll bet you twenty-dollars that you can't make that shot without scratching," exclaimed Bobcat, knowing how impossible a shot like that was to make. Bobcat knew that he could make the shot, but did not know any English that would keep the ball from scratching in the side pocket.

"Bet," said Red.

Red sighted the shot over-and-over again for about five minutes. He looked all around the Nine-Ball. He stroked the stick, but didn't shoot. He got down, putting his eyes almost on the ball, backing away from it slowly, then moving closer to it again. Then he moved along the table with his eyes close to the rag, counting silently. He went around the table and did some kind of diagram with his hands across from where the Nine-Ball laid. Then he smiled at Bobcat.

"Go-head-on, Red, shoot the darn shot. You done called it already," shouted Bobcat, a little annoyed at how long Red was taking to get to the shot.

Bobcat watched Red used very low English. He tapped the cue very easy. It seemed that he did not have enough force behind it to force the Nine-Ball up the table. It slowed up considerably as it crept all the way up the rag, and then, plunked into the corner pocket. The cue bounced slowly around the table and came to rest next to the side pocket, but didn't fall in. It came to rest right where it had contacted the Nine-Ball. "Darn, lucky skunk,"said Bobcat. "That was an impossible shot, man. Let's play for thirty, or nothing, let's see if your luck holds out."

"Got you covered, homes," said Red.

By that evening, Red had cleaned Bobcat out of three-hundred dollars. It was Cat's doubling the bet that did the trick. It got to be right disgusting to Bobcat. The anger in Bobcat's eyes flashed like lightning on the horizon, signaling the coming of a distant storm. Gabe got nervous as Bobcat blinked his eyes, covering up his real feelings with a twisted half-smile.

"Red. Tell the truth. You ain't no country dude from Cismont or Esmont are you?" asked Bobcat. He formed a mean sneer on his face that trailed off into a hateful grin.

"No, Money," said Red. "I came down here with my Crew. See all those country-looking cats hanging in this hall, they're my slack. We're from Northwest Washington, D.C. We're in with the 'Deuce!' We're carrying on the fight up in D.C., dig? We aren't just down here hustling you guys, man. We use the money we cop on programs to help feed and educate our homies up the way. We run clinics, give free-lunches to schoolchildren, and buy groceries for some poor families. So, you ain't been just hustled, really. You have just made a contribution to the cause, slick," said Red. A Forty-Five Automatic's handle was visible through his clothes.

Bobcat was dumbfounded. His angry stare mellowed into a sorrowful glance.

"Look, homes, I'll stick around for a few days or so. If you want a chance to win your money back, I'm down with that. I ain't trying to be nasty like that with any of my Black brothers, man," said Red.

"I'm going to get another stake and come right back. I know I can hang with you on that pool table. I just need another chance to shoot-it-out with you, dude," said Bobcat. He was out the door into the barbershop, then out onto Main Street, leaving the complex by the back way. James and Bubbles left right behind him. *I'm really surprised at that. Bobcat usually gets into a fight before he allows anyone to out-hustle him. It's a pride-of-the-street-thing. He's going out to get some more money to give to that guy from D.C. I always believed that Bobcat had better sense than that, even though he seems crazy at times. Red is a pro when it comes to hustling, and Cat is just going to lose no matter what he tries to do, and that's square-business,* thought Gabe. When Gabe left the complex, he saw a terrible thing going down. He hid behind a tall hedge to listen. Two cops were knocking on Bubbles' door, banging on it like they wanted to tear it down. One of them was yelling something.

"Sophia! Sophia Quayles! This is the police! We want to ask your son a few questions," one of the cops shouted.

A squeaky voice called out from behind the door. "Hold on. Y'all hold on a minute. Hold your horses till I get my bunny slippers on," an old lady chimed.

"Sophia, we want to talk to your boy, Roy. Is he home?" a deep southern drawl bellowed.

"What's Bubbles done, now?" asked Sophia. Her voice trailed off. "Bubbles, where you going? The law's out there ... Why?" Gabe heard the lady's faint plea.

Bubbles yelled, "Momma, I got to get out of here! They're coming to arrest me! I'm in trouble, momma!" shouted Bubbles.

Gabe could see down a little alleyway behind the house. Bubbles lifted a window back there, barely big enough for him to squeeze through. He made it out. "Ow-ow-ow! Get off me!" went a heavy-voiced southern drawl. "Boy, we got you now. Thought you's getting away, didn't you?"

Officer Bradley Gillen, a big, blond, muscular cop, standing at six-foot tall, with a crewcut, beady little blue eyes, a square chin, and tight jaws, had a terrible full nelson on Bubbles. Bubbles didn't squirm or try to get loose. He knew it would do him no good. Gabe had seen this cop on the beat many times. He was known for his cruelty to Blacks, misusing his billy club often without probable cause.

Officer Gillen gave up the full nelson, to punch Bubbles in the stomach. The lick doubled Bubbles up in a knot on the ground between the alleyway.

"I am the man around here, boy. You cons know that! I got a warrant here for your arrest, boy! Roy Quayles, you're charged with the murder of Stanley Graham Longfellow. Anything you say may be used against you in a court of law. You have the right to have a lawyer present before questioning. If you choose to give up that right, what you say may be used against you. Do you understand your rights, Roy?" said Officer Gillen pointedly. "You stupid … You black buzzard!"

Gillen kicked Bubbles several times in his left side. He just groaned. He knew not to resist. "Yes sir … I knows … my rights," he moaned between kicks.

"I tell you what! See?" Officer Gillen held up a money clip full of greenbacks. "I got some money, here. Want to come try to rob me? Why don't you hit me till I'm out, then come and try to take my money? No, I'm not a weak, helpless, student. That's what you're in the market for, ain't it, boy?" shouted Gillen. He kicked Bubbles a horrible blow, Gabe could almost feel it himself. That had to have broken a rib or something. Great, big, ol' Bubbles, started to cry. Gabe was shocked. Bubbles was lying on the ground brawling like an oversized Baby Hugey.

Great fear shown on Bubbles' face. Officer Gillen ripped out his service revolver, pointed it at Bubbles' head and allowed, "I got the solution to all you people over here on Vinegar Hill. Just give me an excuse, boy. Do something! Do anything! I want you to make a false move, so I can blow your fraggin' brains out! Just give me an excuse, boy!" yelled Officer Gillen. He cocked back the hammer of his revolver, pointed it closer to Bubbles' head.

"Brad, Brad, Brad! Don't go there. Don't let that boy get' ya to do that! That's what the NAACP wants us to do. All we got to do is let the law take its course. That'll kill him just as well. Let's just get his dusty butt over to the Jail," said Officer Minor Pace, a five-foot runt of a cop. He seemed too short to be wearing the blue-and-white uniform of a cop, but there he was. He had the same crewcut on his red hair, and had those same little beady, blue, eyes as Gillen.

Bubbles trembled all over. Gabe could see that he was full of uncontrollable panic. If Bobcat could see him now, Gabe believed he'd grab one of the cops' guns and shoot Bubbles himself. The cops pummeled Bubbles with their billy clubs.

"Please don't kick me in my sides no more, Mr. Police! Y'all got the wrong man. I ain't done nothing at all. I ain't guilty! You just think I is. Let the law decide if I'm guilty. I need a lawyer. I want to go before a judge. Y'all just police's. Y'all ain't got no right to kill me," said Bubbles. A hard lick landed on his side again.

"Ow, crap! Ow, that crap hurts!" screamed Bubbles. A crowd of people collected near the alleyway. They had heard Bubbles' screams.

"C'mon, Brad, let's take this sack of do-do over to the Jail and book 'im.

We're getting a crowd. We don't need that," said Officer Pace.

Brad checked Minor and vice-versa, to see if any blood stained their blue-and-white uniforms. They didn't see any. They grabbed Bubbles up off the ground and dragged him out of the alleyway to a patty-wagon parked over on First and Main Northwest, near Bowman's Fish Market. Old man Fitz Bowman was called "The Mayor" of Vinegar Hill. It was a ludicrous title local residents had given him. He was like a white go-between so that whites did not actually have to talk to the Black inhabitants of the Hill. Old man Bowman came to the door of his business to see Sophia's boy carted off like a sack of rotten potatoes. Bubbles being slung into the back of the patty-wagon like a sack of something to discard, groaned loudly as he hit the floor of it. He was handcuffed behind him, and then ankle cuffs got fastened on him too. Gabe couldn't help but feel a little pity for how Bubbles looked.

Gabe mixed with the crowd to get a closer look at Bubbles. He got right near the patty-wagon. He heard Bubbles sobbing hysterically. "They can't prove I done nothing! They got to let me go! … I ain't got nothing to tell you dirty law-dogs…." Bubbles' voice trailed off as the patty-wagon drove away.

Gabe ran towards home that evening like someone being chased. He got a dude along the way to buy him a bottle of whiskey from the ABC store. A pint of

Old Crow. He wanted to drown out the feeling of being a rat-fink. O'Lord, he tried, but failed.

A nervous Gabe sat at the table that morning eating a bowl of oatmeal, thinking, *I heard that they're hiring at the country club up yonder on 250 West. I got to get away from up at the UVA. I can't face George, Sr. I can't face Mrs. Tee. Bobcat, neither.*

A radio broadcast interrupted Gabe's thoughts:

"... Police have arrested two suspects in the murder of Stanley Graham Longfellow. The two suspects are Roy Quayles, called Bubbles, and James Killeen, both from the Vinegar Hill area. A third suspect is still on the loose, police would not give any details or the name of the third person involved in the murder case at this time...."

Gabe dropped his spoon. He ran out of the house, his heart pounded like a drum as he ran along West Main Street. He stopped over near the Safeway grocery store parking lot. He whispered to himself: "Oh, God, what am I going to do, now?

Are the cops talking about Bobcat or me? I can't leave. I can't run away. I'm stuck here. I got to find a way to escape without anyone finding out I was with Bobcat and them the night they killed that student. And I don't want nobody to know I snitched on the Crew either, man."

Gabe didn't know what to do, so he did nothing. He just kept going, putting one feet before the other hoping he'd find a way to go in a different direction one day.

CHAPTER 14

▼

Lieutenant Clemm Doll, the Chief of Homicide Investigations, a swarthy-looking white man, was so dark-skinned, that he seemed very well tanned. His sandy colored hair, big, greenish-blue eyes, and broad nose made him seem like a cross between Abraham Lincoln and Booker T. Washington. The corners of his mouth sloped upwards. His top lip seemed too thick for the average white man's, and more resembled a Black man's lip. But he was allegedly white and very proud of it.

Bubbles stared back at Clemm Doll's big, nervous eyes, seeing nothing but scorn, hatred, viciousness and bloodlust in them. Doll approached Bubbles, to just stand there and war with Bubbles using only his mean stare. Then he spoke in a slow, deliberate, southern drawl.

"Boy, you'coons done made me pret'near tired of fooling'round with y'all. Yeah, I'm tired of y'all jerking me'round!" Doll yelled at Bubbles. He focused the extremely bright interrogation light directly at Bubbles' eyes so that it blinded him.

"You look uncomfortable there, boy. Let me adjust your cuffs a little," said Doll with a cruel sneer forming across his face. He tightened Bubbles handcuffs so tight that they dug into his wrists.

"Ow! Ow! Mr. Doll. Please, man, loosen them things! I can't stand them that tight!" screamed Bubbles.

Doll loosen the cuffs a little. He yelled, "Shoot Roy, boy you ain't seen no pain yet. You might as well relax and enjoy it. Wait till one of them bucks down at the penitentiary gets through with you, pretty-boy, then you'll know what pain is. See, that's where you're headed–you and your friends. You all are going to be somebody's girly-men. You got that?" shouted Doll. A wicked grin came across his tawny face.

Bubbles knew that when they brought him up from that nasty old Jail on Eight Street Northwest to the police precinct station in the Midway Building that it weren't going to be no picnic. Especially with Mr. Doll. That law-dog was crazy as hell, and hated Blacks. Rumor had it, that he'd killed more than one, and that was how he got to be such a big shot cop. He was known as one to help keep the "Niggers," in their place.

The shackles on Bubbles' ankles felt like they weighed a ton. Worst of all, Bubbles could smell his own body odor. No chance to bathe. His gray jail over-alls made him feel miserable, dirty, sticky, and nasty. The shackles had cut sore-rings on his ankles. Every move Bubbles made was very painful.

"Tell me, darkie … Tell me what I want to know! Tell me about your part in the bludgeoning to death of that student up at the University. Now, you know something about that! One of your friends done informed on y'all! Don't lie!" screamed Doll. He slapped Bubbles so hard that his ears rung. It made Bubbles' whole head hurt. No response from Bubbles infuriated Doll even more. Red streaks came across his face. "Stand-up! You get up from there!" screamed Doll.

Soon as Bubbles scrambled up to his feet, Doll kicked him in his scrotum. It sent a wave of convulsive pain throughout Bubbles' body. "Oh, hell! … Ow-w-w-w-w! Uh-uh-uh-uh! Ow-ow-ow!" screamed Bubbles, lying knotted up on the floor as much as his shackles and handcuffs would allow.

"Mr. Doll! You didn't have to do that crap!" shouted Bubbles. Sour smelling puke gushed out of his mouth. Doll jumped back out of the way to keep it from getting on his white shirt and red tie, his tan slacks and or his brown wingtips. Instinctively, he put his right hand on the pearl handle of his Forty-five snub-nosed revolver, hanging in a left-side shoulder holster.

"Get up off that floor, boy—right now!" ordered Doll. "And I bet you better be about it quick!"

"Yes sir," said Bubbles. Although his body was wracked with pain, he stumbled up to his knees, then lifted himself up to the chair he had been seated in. He plumped down in the chair, with tears easing down his cheeks.

"I want the dope on the killer or killers of the young man up at the University, 'Buggy, Bobo, Bubbles,' or whatever they call you, Roy! And I'm going to get-it-the-hell-out-of-you! If you didn't kill that student, you know who did. 'Nigger!' you going to tell me, too!" said Clemm. "I got ways to get at the truth you ain't never dreamed about, boy!" screamed Detective Clemm Doll. "Now get the hell out of my face 'less you want to confess, or tell me what I want to know."

He stood up pointing his right index finger at Bubbles menacingly without saying a word, cursing Roy Quayles to death with his eyes.

Two blue-and-white rookies grabbed Bubbles up and nearly dragged him out of the interrogation room. Bubbles uttered under his breath, "I hope the boys catch your racist ass out one night and cut your fraggin' throat. I hope I be with them when it happens." His eyes were a bloodshot mess, his wrists ached, his balls swollen, and his ankles were one huge pain. He was taken back to Jail, wishing he was dead.

On the next morning, Detective Doll, Officers Gillen and Pace stood before James Killeen's cell at the Jail. He had been picked up right after Bubbles' arrest. He didn't know what had happen to his main-man, Bubbles, but the screaming coming from his cell was annoying as hell. James had just been mildly shoved around.

James figured that they must be ready to work him over some more now. He could see the evil gleam in the cops' eyes. All of them were snarling at him like a pack of dogs does at a cornered cat. James ran to the farthest corner of his cell, and squeezed into it as tightly as he could. He had nowhere else to run. He threw up his hands.

"What y'all go do to me now? What? ... What the heck y'all looking at me like that for?" yelled James like a hysterical person in a scream-flick. "I just know you mo-joe's ain't go pull no funny stuff with me, James. Look ... you got the wrong man!" The chains on James' ankles jingled as he balled up his knees to his chin, hoping that he'd awake from this bad dream and it would all be over.

Doll took out his ring of keys, slowly, eyeing James, staring at him like a maddened Grizzly Bear. He inserted one of the keys into an electric lock. James' cell door slammed opened.

"No-o-o-o! You honkey mo-joe's, y'all's just wrong! You got the wrong man! I ain't guilty of nothing at all," shouted James. The cops came into the cell rushing at him, making him feel like a rabbit cornered by the hounds after a hot chase.

"Shut up! Boy, it's too late for you!" Doll yelled. He ran right over to James, kicked him in the groin, and in the mouth, and up beside his head several times. He got into a frenzy on James.

The pain was so intense that James' mouth hung open without him making a sound. A silent scream is all that he was able to emit. Then James whispered through bloody lips, "I ain't ... done ... nothing ..." followed by unintelligible shrieks and screams that made no sense.

Doll ranted and raved at James, "'Coon-Nigger! You're looking death in the face!" he shouted. His voice got louder and louder. "Shut up! Shut up! We're going to get to the bottom of this crap and I mean today! We believe that you and your darky-sidekicks beat, robbed and killed that student up at the University. You stained Rugby Road with his blood. The blood of a white man. All of y'all is going to pay for that, boy!"

All three cops took turns kicking James, like they were kicking a soccer ball. Pace yelled between kicks, "We want all you coloreds out of the downtown area, you're polluting it!"

Gillen yelled, "The best darn 'Nigger,' is a dead 'Nigger!' and I want to make good ones out of all y'all on Vinegar Hill! If you ask me, you're all guilty of killing that student!"

Gillen grabbed his police revolver out of a holster on his hip, cocked it and aimed it at an almost unconscious human-heap lying on the Jail floor, wallowing in his piss, his dung, and his vomit. James heard a faint voice utter, "No, that's not the way, the time, nor the place! …"

James came to lying in his own mess. He dragged himself up off the floor, tried to clean himself as best he could without a towel, washcloth, or soap. He used the one roll of toilet paper in his cell, cold water and his cuffed-hands. The putrid smell of his crap and vomit permeated throughout the cell and probably the entire cellblock.

"I hurt everywhere. My whole body is one huge pain. I wish they had gone on and shot me. My balls feel like little sacks of water full of pain," moaned James. The pain was too much for his brain to comprehend, so it caused him to fall into a fitful sleep. He fainted.

Doll and company went straight-away to Bubbles' cell. Doll opened the cell door. Bubbles seeing them coming for him tried to ball up under his bunk bed. His lips trembled as the Officers towered over him. Great terror came into his eyes.

Bubbles felt the pain caused by a billy club being cracked solidly on his head. He fell unconscious to the floor. He had no feelings for a while after that.

Both Bubbles and James came to in the same cell.

"I'm hurt real bad … My butt even aches, them mo-joe's whipped the crap out of me, kicked me in the balls, and now I may never be able to make babies, man,"whined James. He discovered that he was unshackled, and uncuffed. He limped across the clean cell to a sink, just above the toilet stool, got hold of a large bar of Ivory Soap, one of two white washcloths, and towels, and got busy getting out of his soiled overalls. Both he and Bubbles had clean overalls lying on their bunk beds. James wasted no time getting cleaned up.

"Me too. They knocked me out like a light, man. They must've kicked me in the balls several times while I was lying on that floor knocked out. I'll get even with them if it's the last thing I do," said Bubbles. "This place is the nastiest place in the world, James." He took his turn scrubbing as best he could with cold water.

"You know though, man. Bobcat ain't been down here to see about us. He didn't send none of the home-boys, neither. If I didn't know better, I'd think our boy done forgot about us, James," said Bubbles. He threw up his hands in exasperation.

James raised his right hand. "Look, Bubbles. Don't get excited, man. Don't freak out. Homey's just waiting till things cool down. Y'know, he knows he owes us, big-time. Bubbles, I'm going through too much for Bobcat to forget about me. Why, if I thought he was about to do that, I'd rat that mo-joe out, man," he whined.

"I don't want to go to no prison," said Bubbles. "That's really bad news."

James' face took on the image of a scared little boy. Bubbles, did you get raped down at Hanover, man?" he asked.

"James, we all got raped down at Hanover. You know that, man—even Cat did, too," said Bubbles. "But that don't make no punk out of you, so hold tight, man—dig?"

"I don't want that to happen to me again, bro. If we testify for the State, Bobcat will get the chair. We can make a deal with the law or something! ..." James blurted out.

Bubbles stared at James with venomous anger in his face. "James, that crap you're talking is making me madder than a mo-joe! You scared, chicken-crap, sucker! You acting worst than Gabe. You s'pose to be one of the roughest, fighting-est walk-partners out there. Now you up in here ready to cheese-out Bobcat," shouted Bubbles, then he slapped James hard across the face.

"Look, James, one of the homies already down the road will cut our throats if we rat Bobcat out. Prison can't save us, dude. Just keep your mouth shut. Man, they ain't really got nothing on us. If they don't do something soon, we'll be allowed to walk. If they truly had anything, we'd be gone already—you know the deal," said Bubbles. "So, keep yourself together."

James was too panicky to be easily reasoned with. "But Bubbles, all Bobcat had to do was knockout that student. He didn't have to go showing off like that, talking about he's some 'African Warrior, or Prince' or something. Now, look at the trouble we're in. His butt ain't even been arrested yet. I wonder about that Bubbles," whined James. "Bobcat is the killer, not us."

Bubbles hit James a lick harder than any one of the cops had. He was knocked down. "Shut up, James! You know the cops probably got this cell bugged, man. You might've just given away the whole caper!"

James exclaimed, "I didn't mean to … I didn't think about that crap. Man, you may be right. Why else would they put us in the same cell after a ferocious beating? They probably figured we'd talk about things … I mean … man we could be in a lot of trouble." James' voice trembled as did his whole body.

"James, don't talk to me no more. Long as they keep us locked up together, be quiet about things–you dig?" pled Bubbles.

The trusties came with the evening meal. Bubbles and James had gotten used to dry cornbread, and water, cornflakes with thick cream or cold, pasty oatmeal, cold fishcakes, stale buttermilk and little else. But standing in front of their cell were foods that made their digestive juices flow: Fried Chicken, Mashed Potatoes and Gravy, Collard Greens, Sweet Rolls, and Chocolate Cake. The usual buttermilk or warmish water was not being served, but a pitcher of Ice-Cold Cool Aid. Two trays piled-high were shoved into their cell. It dumbfounded them.

Both men forgot about what James had said. They were starved, so they stuffed themselves. The satisfaction of their hunger left room for them to reflect on the situation at hand.

"James, why you think we's getting such special treatment?" asked Bubbles. "I don't know, man. I hope it ain't because–you know?–they done heard the rap and got it in for us. I'll be so glad when we get out of here, man." He rubbed his rough, unshaven face. It made him grimace at how greasy and sticky it felt.

A grinning trusty came for their steel trays and drinking cups.

"I wonder what the heck he's smiling at us like that for?" said Bubbles. "That white mo-joe knows something, though. We ain't got diddly to bribe him with to find out what he knows."

"You know though man, I'd just like to know why we ain't been allowed as much as a phone call?" said James. "We just been in this Jail like we were already convicted or something. Man, we know what the blues is all about."

Huge roaches crawling all over the walls of their cell made Bubbles' skin crawl. The whole place was nothing but a living nightmare for him. He hoped that Bobcat was appreciating what he and James went through for his cock-strong butt!

"Lamb-sakes, Lennie! By-gum! We got them Black rascals, now!" Doll blurted into the phone's receiver. "We can switch the system off, now. I done heard who killed that student up at the University; and, we's right, it was one of them

Hill-Rats from over yonder on Vinegar Hill." Doll chuckled like a little kid winning at marbles.

"Chief Moon, we just got to figure a way to even things with them boys, and at the same time, remove the 'Nigger' horde away from downtown. I know you get where I'm coming from," said Doll.

"Yeah, Clemm, old buddy, I'm with you more than one-darn-hundred percent! I'm going to call a special meeting with you and I, and officials from up at the University. We got to get our heads together on this one. Maybe this is the break we all been waiting for, but we're going to need a lot of cooperation," exclaimed Moon.

"We got to get the 'Nigs' as far away from Vinegar Hill as possible. We don't want them living anywhere near Main Street ever again. Clemm, good buddy, I don't want to ever see one of their dusty butts 'less it's here cleaning City Hall," said Moon.

"I got you. See you later, then, Lennie," said Doll. He hung up the phone.

Pace, Doll, and Gillen were overjoyed at their accomplishment. Doll pulled a Fifth of Cutty Sark Scotch out of a desk drawer. He produced three shot glasses. He poured liquor into each one.

"Here Brad. Here Minor," he said, handing a glass to one then the other. "Here's to the removal of a whole doggone 'Nigger' neighborhood," said Doll.

They all tapped glasses and gulped down the liquor, then cheered.

CHAPTER 15

▼

Gabe could've sworn that a dude was following him as he hurried from the Lafayette Theater, located on the triangle at Second, and First Streets and Preston Avenue. *I hope Bubbles and James don't call my name. I don't want to be involved in their crap. And, why haven't the cops picked up Bobcat?* wondered Gabe as he strode along Third Street. It was good and dark outside and Gabe was nervous walking the streets alone these days.

Gabe wondered: *How did Vinegar Hill get to be so slummy? There are a lot of beautiful homes over on the Hill. Why are thy still over here among the slums? How did so many affluent Black people get trapped on the Hill? I'm really going to find out the answer to these questions. I know people who work up at the Alderman Library at the UVA. They can get me books to read, and old newspaper clippings of editorials from the Daily Progress, that go way back. I want to know! ...* thought Gabe.

Being afraid to hang around the streets, Gabe spent most of his free time reading and now, taking notes, from the books and materials he studied. He soaked up every bit of knowledge he could find out about Charlottesville, Vinegar Hill, and the people who had lived on the Hill before Nineteen-Sixty-Three.

Gabe discovered that Vinegar Hill in Charlottesville, Virginia was so named by Irish Immigrants who had settled there in the early 1800s. Near where there is a statue depicting the Lewis and Clark expedition, in the middle of a concourse where West Main, Ridge, McIntire and Garret Streets now conjoin, in the early 1800s, stood a public watering trough, and pump, used to water horses. Various Clans of the Irish would have mud-wallowing fights there whenever they met.

The feuds went back into ancient Irish history, and were as bitter as vinegar, thus the name, "Vinegar Hill."

Newspaper accounts had it that Irish Immigrants smuggled liquor into town in large wooden casks marked as vinegar. One day several of the casks fell off the wagon and burst asunder. These were actually filled with vinegar. The putrid smell lingered in the air for weeks, and this is where the name, "Vinegar Hill," came from.

Welsh Winston, in his research, stated that, "It was at Vinegar Hill in Ireland that an agrarian revolt took place in 1789. 'Vinegar Hill' was a fighting song of both the Catholic and Protestant troops. In the early Nineteenth Century the Irish brought the name 'Vinegar Hill' over with them to Charlottesville, where once again, a 'Hill' had become an Irish battleground."

Welsh went further, he says, "A hotel called the 'Farmers Hotel' stood across from a rival tavern. The patrons of the rival tavern would get drunk and then brawls would breakout being pushed and edged-on by onlookers.

"The brawlers had names like 'O'Toole, O'Tracy, and O'Doll, who were cousins to the O'Donovans, McPaces, and McGillens. These families owned most of the restaurants, hotels and taverns on what they came to call, 'Vinegar Hill.'

"Old man O'Toole allegedly named the 'Hill' in honor of Ireland's 'Vinegar Hill.' He was a thriving Tailor, and the Irish 'Vinegar Hill' was his ancestral home."

A friend of Gabe's found an old tattered manuscript in the Alderman Library Rare Book Division. He was a janitor up there, and was able to borrow the material for a few days without it being missed. It stated that, "an earlier name for what became 'Vinegar Hill' was 'Random Row.' It was located on land owned by a farmer named Joseph Bishop. Houses were constructed on the 'Hill' in a haphazard, random manner. Other town-dwellers came to refer to the area as 'that, random row,' and eventually, 'Random Row' was incorporated into the Town of Charlottesville in 1835. It was the oldest part of 'Vinegar Hill,' and many ex-slaves had built homes there."

So, that's where the name "Vinegar Hill" came from, and why "Random Row" was so ghost-like, and crumbling down to the ground, thought Gabe.

Welsh Winston's research further revealed to Gabe, "That in the 1850s waves of the Irish, Scots, Germans, and Jews came to Charlottesville and the Albemarle County area. Many thousands of these immigrants spent a very short time in the area. They were on their way to other areas like West Virginia, Pennsylvania, Washington, D.C., Delaware, and Maryland. Still others went on to New York,

New Jersey, and Chicago. The Charlottesville area was in fact being tested by them to see if it was a suitable place to settle…. Those who stayed in the area had among them entrepreneurs who founded prosperous businesses like tailoring shops, barbershops, grocery stores, hotels, taverns and fine restaurants. For the gentry, they founded fine, clothing stores, tanneries and carriage-making shops, blacksmith shops, boutiques, and shoe stores. On Vinegar Hill, a gentleman or lady could buy or have imported anything his or her heart desired. Most immigrants who came to Charlottesville were not rich, nor of the gentry, and were in fact borderline 'gutter-rats.' They mixed freely with slaves and free Blacks, up until the Fugitive Slave Act of the 1850s.

"After the founding of the University of Virginia in 1819 by Thomas Jefferson, the son of Irish Immigrants, a motel was constructed on the Hill for an Alexander Garret, the Court Clerk for Albemarle County. It was where the noblest members of the gentry lodged when they brought their young gentlemen to be enrolled at the University of Virginia. It eventually became the Midway Building where City Hall had set up shop."

Gabe realized that, *The Midway Building, that's where ol' Vera Works. Now ain't that some coincidence?*

Winston's research further enlightened Gabe. "The Midway Building was completed in 1828, and was a two-story edifice resembling a very large rectangle of bricks and mortar, with several gabled windows, and roof to match."

In 1963, the Midway Building was just about the same as it started out, excepting that it had been renovated in the interior, thought Gabe.

In another piece of Winston's research, Gabe discovered, "that by the 1850s, most of the early well-to-do Immigrants had moved off Vinegar Hill to Albemarle, Nelson, Fluvanna, Madison, Greene and Buckingham Counties. They populated places like Shadwell, Cismont, Esmont, North Gardens, Schuyler, Earlysville, Scottsville, New Canton, Arvonia, Bermo Bluff, Troy, Covesville, Standardsville and Columbia. Many founded splendid plantations as did Nathaniel Greene, Thomas Jefferson, James Madison, and James Monroe.

"Lesser members of the gentry established smaller plantations. Such were the O'Dolls. They had run a lucrative leather-goods store on Vinegar Hill. But by the 1850s, they were able to move out to Earlysville, situated at about fifteen miles Northwest of Charlottesville. The slave trade had become so attractive to John Farley O'Doll, that he had constructed a fine Jeffersonian-styled Mansion in the middle of a seventy-seven acre spread out near the Town of Earlysville. Wealth beckoned!

"He moved his beautiful satin-blond wife, Sue Ellen, his daughter, Mary Elizabeth, and John, Jr., out to their new home in 1849. John was a very handsome man. His wife complemented his good looks with her own. John, Jr., was the spitting image of his doting father, but Mary Beth was the 'Ugly Duckling' of the family. She was the oldest of the children. John, Jr., was twenty in 1849, and Mary Beth was twenty-five. She was thought by her peers to be 'an old spinster.'

"One of the twelve slaves purchased by John, Sr., was a handsome mulatto that answered to the name of 'Hitter,' because of his cruelty to the other slaves. He was 'Mas'er John's' slave driver. 'Hitter,' also had what he called his 'Christian name.' It was 'Moses.'

"For eleven years, the O'Dolls prospered on their plantation, raising corn, tobacco, wheat, barley, cattle and horses. Everything they ate was grown on their farms. Then the Civil War broke out. The day came when John and John, Jr., who had married the daughter of their neighbor, Gerald McPace, Betty Louise McPace, got on two of the best white horses the plantation had produced and rode off to join their comrades in a 'War to save their homeland, the South, and to preserve one of its God-sanctioned institutions, slavery.'

"As 'Mas'er John' rode away 'Hitter' promised, 'I'll keep your place just like it is till you gets back, sir.'

"'That's a good boy, Hitter,'"replied John, Sr. He and his son soon rounded the curve on their way to Richmond, Virginia. They wore the gray uniforms of the Confederacy.

"Two years into the War, most of John Farley O'Doll's slaves ran away. Only 'Hitter' and Unc' Willie, an old field hand too feeble to run, and Matilda, a mulatto house servant, somewhere in her late teens to early twenties, stayed with the O'Doll family.

"No word from John or his son, filled their women left behind with dread. As resources became as scarce as hen-teeth, and there were no slaves to do the hard work, everything started to fall apart. Like their neighbors, the O'Dolls just dragged through life clinging to as much of their opulent past lives as they could. They had very little to put on fine china, but they set the tables as though a full meal was being served. Even went through the trouble of dressing for dinner. Sometimes, all that the whole household had for supper was some soup made from whatever vegetables the slaves could forage that day. The farms were soon overgrown and the whole plantation looked rundown. Sue Ellen and Betty Lou fell into a state of deep depression. They withdrew from the horrible realities surrounding them.

"'Hitter' was a mix of the white slave master of the Joseph Coles' plantation in Western Albemarle and Lizzy Ann his beautiful mulatto cook. He had reddish, kinky, hair, orange-colored skin, bright-green eyes, and was built like Atlas. His slightly broad nose was the only part of him that tied him inexplicably to Africa. Except for his continued hateful gaze, he was a handsome individual.

"Mary Beth ordered 'Hitter' to the Big House one day in 1864 and seduced him and promised to marry him after the South lost the War. She figured it would have to end that way, because the South didn't have enough resources to defeat the North, and even she could see that. She even moved Moses into a room of the Mansion, not fearing anything, because she figured that her father and brother were lost out there on some battlefield, like at Antietam, Chancellorsville, Gettysburg, Petersburg, or Richmond. Four years had passed and not even a letter had made it through to home to tell them of their whereabouts and general condition.

"Her physique was slightly hunch-shouldered. She was short and duffy, had acme, and a long, hooked nose. Two thin lips were like lines across her face. She was not very desirable or attractive at all. The young bachelors in her class would not even think of courting her, not even for a good inheritance. So Mary Beth grew lonelier and lonelier as she grew older. She hoped that 'Hitter' would favor white women enough to make love to her. She found out that she was right. He did enjoy what she offered him, time and time again.

"On this morning, a Private, wearing a Confederate uniform stood knocking on the front door of the O'Dolls' Big House. Matilda, the house girl, a shapely, voluptuous, 'gal,' with tan skin, light-brown eyes, and long, black, Indian-braids hanging down her back, standing at five-foot tall, came to answer the door. She wore a light-blue gingham dress, with a white apron over that.

"'Let me speak with Mrs. Sue Ellen O'Doll and Mrs. Betty Lou O'Doll, gal,' said the one-arm, soldier.

"'I'll go get them, sir,' said Matilda.

"Sue Ellen and Betty Lou came to the front door sort of holding on to each other, trembling and crying knowing to expect the worst. Many families had gotten the same kind of news.

"'Hello, ladies. I'm Private Wendell Shelburne. I'm sorry to have to tell you fine people that Capt'n John Farley O'Doll, Sr., died bravely at the 'Battle of the Crater' in Petersburg, Virginia. Lieutenant John Farley O'Doll, Jr., was killed by a cowardly Yankee Sniper, just yesterday. May God bless you one and all. The bodies of our fallen dead is not recoverable at this time, but as soon as possible, we will return the remains of our gallant boys to their home soil. Good day, ma'am.'

"Just like that the man was gone. Sue Ellen melted down into an emotional heap on the plush carpets of her home. She died right there of a heart attack. Betty Lou went quietly into the barn and hung herself from the low-rafters. She left two girls behind, four-year old twins, Julia and Janice. Mary Beth had to raise them.

"After discovering that John, Jr., was not going to return from the War, Matilda ran away immediately. Said she was going North. She was never heard from again. Unc' Willie just walked away from the plantation, just kept on going in search of the wife and children 'Mas'er Robert Epps of Shadwell' had sold to some plantation in the Tidewater area. All he'd heard was that it was the biggest spread around them parts. War, or no War, he wanted to find his wife Cora, his sons, Bradley, and Madison, and his baby-child, Lillian. Hadn't seen them in ten years.

"Mary Beth made Moses keep his hair cut short, and his face shaved clean, so that he could pass for white. In his clothes, he resembled a dark-skinned Irishman. In time Moses and Mary Beth had nine children, all boys. Two of her boys, the older two, Winston and Carlston, eventually married Janice and Julia Doll. Mary Beth had dropped the 'O' from their name. From these marriages, a Doll clan sprung up. Each son fathered ten children with their cousins. The children of these married into the Gillen, Pace and Moon families. The 'Mc' had been dropped from everyone's name.

"The Hinter farm was in Western Albemarle near Lexington. They eventually dated and or courted girls all over the Charlottesville area. The slave master of this farm fathered a horde of children by slave women. Many Blacks on Vinegar Hill were descended from this notorious slave master or one of his sons. One such descendant was George Washington Hinter, Sr., Bobcat's father. Bubbles and James were also descendent from such unions as well … and, they very well knew about this."

It dawned on Gabe very heavily: *So, that's what was wrong with Clemmon Doll, Minor Pace and Bradley Gillen. They were afraid of being kin to 'Niggers!' The one-drop-rule meant that if they had one drop of Black blood in their veins, that made them just as much a 'Nigger!' as me. The crackers around here are all afraid of finding out that they are really Black.*

The fact that Welsh Winston had found out about their little secret had to have put his life in danger. Now, I got to wonder did something awful happen to him for real. I'm a ask Mrs. Hinter to see if she knows.

The record that Welsh Winston had left behind showed Gabe, "that in the 1860s, after the Civil War had ended, a number of Black people opened businesses on Vinegar Hill. Blacks and whites ran their shops, restaurants, and motels on the opposite sides of the streets. Often, Blacks owned businesses that did not cater to Blacks. Most whites owning businesses that catered to Blacks, hired Blacks to run those businesses. In other cases, whites rented buildings and properties that they owned to Blacks. Most Blacks owning businesses rented from white absentee landlords.

"As more Blacks moved into Vinegar Hill, the more whites moved out, leaving behind vacant dwellings. When the whites absenting themselves from Vinegar Hill rented properties to Blacks, they let the rental properties go to ruin, mainly because they were 'just renting to the Niggers.'

"By the 1950s, the buildings being rented to Blacks showed little sign that the property owners had made any effort to modernize their rental properties. That is why most dwellings in 1963 were still without electricity, indoor plumbing, or restrooms, nor central heat, and seemed like rundown hovels on the outside...."

Vinegar Hill had become a smelly slum by 1963, Gabe could see that for himself. On the outside of most homes on the Hill, houses looked terrible to the onlookers; but, Gabe saw, as in the case of Vera's and Bubbles' houses, that Black people had made their hovels very liveable inside. It was like walking into a barn to find yourself standing in a mansion. That is what was unique about Vinegar Hill. The problem is, though, *Most people saw only the eye-sore that the Hill had become on the outside, and not its distinguishing characteristics to the contrary on the inside. That is why most whites in power saw Vinegar Hill as an unredeemable slum,* concluded Gabe.

A newspaper article, probably out of Charlottesville's only Black newspaper, stated that "By 1963, Blacks owned thirty businesses on Vinegar Hill to just fifteen owned by whites. The businesses Blacks owned included a motel, tailor shops, barbershops, several restaurants, pool halls, shoe shops, several dance halls, and several musical instrument and repair shops, and record stores." Gabe was enlightened about what Vinegar Hill was, but puzzled about who Welsh Winston was.

I've got to find out what really happened to Welsh Winston. I want to know a lot more about this intelligent man. Why didn't he get his manuscript published? Why don't Mrs. Tee or old George try to get this important work by Welsh Winston published? Why does Mrs. Tee talk about putting this man's great work out for trash pickup? What's everybody so scared of about this man? I'm a ask her the very next chance I get. I've got to hear the rest of the story, thought Gabe.

CHAPTER 16

▼

On this morning, Gabe decided to take off from work to talk to Mrs. Tee. She came strutting down the little hallway to her bathroom. Gabe cracked his door open. It startled Mrs. Tee. She didn't realize there was anyone still in the house. She was wearing a pink, sheer, peekaboo, negligee. She ran back to her bedroom in a flash.

"Oh ... I didn't know nobody was home," said Mrs. Tee with a gleeful chuckle. "I'm sorry, honey."

"No. No. I didn't see a thing," lied Gabe.

Mrs. Tee had put on one of her colorful Egyptian-styled housecoats. She sat down at the kitchen table. "Want a cup of coffee, Gabe?" she asked.

"Don't mind if I do," replied Gabe.

She got up from the table, moseyed over to the stove, got the black pot of per-colating coffee, poured out some into two ivy-cups, and asked, "how do you take yours, honey?"

"Two spoons of sugar and two daubs of cream," said Gabe with a smile on his lips.

"Well, there you go," said Mrs. Tee, as she handed him a cup of hot coffee.

"What's on your mind, son?" she asked. She could see the puzzlement on his face.

Gabe took a careful sip of his coffee. "Who was Welsh Winston? ... I mean ... Who was he, really?" asked Gabe nervously sipping out of his cup of coffee.

"Gabe, now that you have been renting over here for a while, I may as well drop the whole story on you. This is some heavy crap, now Gabe," said Mrs. Tee demurely.

"What? Why! ..." replied Gabe.

"No, son. You got to listen. A lot of things on your mind, and that are happening around here will make a lot more sense if you pick up on this story. It's not a story, actually. It's what happened to a very decent man," said Mrs. Tee.

Gabe just shook his head from side to side.

"Gabe ... Welsh Winston and Bill Griot were the same person," said Mrs. Tee, pausing for a couple of seconds to gauge the shock on Gabe's young face. She drained her first cup of coffee, got up, poured herself another, came and plopped down at the table again.

"Yes, Gabriel. Welsh Winston was the pen name Bill Griot was going to use when he got around to finishing the book he was planning to get published. He'd been a high schoolteacher over at Jefferson when that school got closed and most of the Black teachers were laid-off. He was one of the unfortunate, brilliant though he was. He went over to Burley but decided to quit after hearing that that school was going to fire all of its Black teachers and become a middle school. He'd had all that he could stand. He quit and got a grant to write a book.

"So he decided to write a history of Vinegar Hill, and race relations in Charlottesville to see if he'd be able to find out another way to fit into the new scheme of things. He made the mistake of stumbling onto some local history that became an all-out obsession with him. He said to me one day, 'Tee, I believe that any number of whites–almost all of them around here–in this city and its surrounding counties are very close-kin to Black people. I have discovered a way to start tracing the kinship histories of quite a few whites who are directly descended from Black-white unions....'

"Gabe, he was fine until he went up to Dolls' Hollow, asking around, about some very unsettling facts. He'd heard that Clemmon Doll's great, great, great, grandfather was Moses Doll. He was an ex-slave–a Negro–Gabe. See, that would make Clemm Doll a Negro or 'Nigger!' no matter how white he looks now," said Mrs. Tee. She had a little smirk on her pretty lips. Her hands trembled a little.

"So, that's what a lot of the hatred is all about. It's just another fear," said Gabe. "Like the White Whale in 'Moby Dick,' and whatnot," he allowed.

"Yeah. That's somewhat it, honey. Pardon me, while I go get me another cup of java," said Mrs. Tee. She got another cup of coffee, poured in a lot of cream, three spoons of sugar, stirred it all up, took a sip, and pranced on back to the table.

"Baby, Minor Pace and Bradley Gillen are cousins to Clemmon Doll. They are kin to Moses Doll too. You know, the 'One-Drop-Rule,' that makes them a little less than white, now! They can't change the past, but they don't want nobody to know about their real bloodline either," said Mrs. Tee.

Gabe's eyes were almost squinted shut from the shock of the news he was hearing.

"Back awhile ago, Detective Doll came by here a number of times to talk with Bill Griot. Right in that room there where you rent, they yelled at one another, barking like dogs. Doll cursed the old guy out. He allowed one day, 'It ain't never going to see the light of day, nohow!' to Bill. As he was leaving, he kicked the door to old Bill's bedroom almost off the hinges. As he stormed out of the room, I heard Clemm shout, 'I'll stop you nosy 'Nigger!' if it's the last thing I do!'

"Honey, a couple of weeks later, they found Bill Griot balled up in a heap on old Random Row. He was swollen up with no scars on his outward body. Mack Wine had been poured all over him. So, on the radio and in the papers, they said he drank himself to death, after he found out that he might not have another contract that Fall, because the schools had to be desegregated by then, and that was by order of the Supreme Court. Bull-crap! Don't believe it, Gabe!

"Their claim that Bill Griot died from alcohol poisoning is a darn lie, Gabe. George and I believe that the cops beat that man with rubber hoses, and then covered that up by pouring Mack Wine all over him. I think they dumped his body over on Random Row where the winos hangout, after killing him somewhere else," said Mrs. Tee. Tears came into her beautiful eyes. She got a tissue to blow her nose.

"I never did see Bill Griot take a drink of anything, let alone, that nasty old Mack Wine, the cheapest swill out there—next to Boar's Head Apple and whatnot. Them cops just murdered him to shut him up, that's all," whined Mrs. Tee.

"That's a low-down dirty-shame!" said Gabe, raising his voice to an emphatic level.

"What can you do, Gabe, when the law's doing the dirty work? Who do you turn to then?" Mrs. Tee asked Gabe, earnestly.

"I'on'know," said Gabe, shaking his head for emphasis. "Black people are in deep do-do these days. I can see, now, why you didn't put them papers out for trash pickup. Hell, they might've got you next, because they got to be afraid that you're going to finish Bill Griot's book," said Gabe, with his voice full of excitement. Then Gabe scratched his head.

Them white people will kill to coverup the fact that Blacks in their areas are more than likely just as close-kin to them as the whites. It's that old segregation crap again! Blacks have different hair types—for the most part—and other racial characteristics that distinguish them from so-called whites. But, in reality, the whites know there is not a bit of difference between a Black person and a white one. They are all Human Beings. But a sane person has to invent a reason to kill a fellow Human Being. So, white people have invented the word 'Nigger!' to circumvent any realization that Black people are fellow Human Beings, and are their close-kin Black relatives, reasoned Gabe, in deep thought for a second or two.

"Yeah, sure you're right, Gabe," said Mrs. Tee.

Gabe got up from the table, and went back to the room where Bill Griot had spent his last days. Then it dawn on him: *I got to face it. I seen Old Bill's ghost up at the bus terminal on the bus. It's incumbent upon me to take what wisdom this man's disquieted spirit tried to impart unto me. That's how my mother would want me to think. The ghost warned me to not let fear govern my actions, because such fears in Doll, Pace and Gillen had prompted them to murder in order to coverup the truth. What I'm still confused about is why did the ghost of Bill Griot pick me to speak to? What could he have meant when he said, "When you are filled with wonder about this place, just ask around for old William Griot, and somebody will know where to find me?"*

Sitting in his room at the desk where Bill Griot had worked, Gabe reflected on the situation some more: *Maybe, Bill Griot was killed by Doll, Gillen and Pace so fast, that his soul still wanders around on Vinegar Hill. He is very unwilling to accept death. Could be that his soul is resisting leaving the Hill and the Ville, till his killers meet a just end. His soul just can't rest. Oh, boy. What a day this has been,* thought Gabe as darkness crept over the city of Charlottesville.

Gabe sat quietly at the supper table that evening not hardly eating a thing. His mind was in a semi-dream state. Mrs. Tee, knowing that she had put a lot on his young mind, left him to his thoughts. Then, Gabe retired to his room.

The darkness of the night came with an eerie tint to it. Once in bed, the heaviness of Gabe's eyes gave way to a deep sleep.

"Gabe, Gabe, Gabe! ..." He seemingly was wide awake and was standing on the corner of Random Row and Fourth Streets. William Griot came up out of a heap of trash or something. He was wearing the same pants, shirt and tennis he had previously worn on the bus. Except now, his hair and beard were long and bright-white. His face had a sunlight-like aura around it. His ghost shown like the sun at noonday. His voice sounded like the rushing of a great waterfall. When he uttered his words, lightning lit-up the horizon and thunder rolled, peal after loud peal. Gabe's body felt like running, but he was frozen in-place.

"Now that you've heard the past, and experienced the present, go and hear the future. I have given you the keys to understanding. You must unlock the doors to knowledge yourself. Within them are treasures that many men long to have, but few

ever possess. The wisdom acquired by the whole of mankind throughout the ages is the greatest treasure on earth.

"Now go!" said the ghost of William Griot. "I bid you God's Speed, go!" he shouted, as the wind blew exceeding hard until it moaned like a dying man. A magnificently-bright, very large cloud came out of the sky with an oscillating red-to-yellow light in its middle. It descended down and round about William Griot. "You will not see me again, Gabe. You are now 'A Messenger!' That's what your name means. Now, go and tell the story!

"You are going to witness terrible and horrible things. It is your plight. Embrace it. Do Not Run From It!" Then the cloud engulfed old Bill....

Gabe awoke. It was morning. His body felt very hot and sweaty. He trembled all over, afraid, but not knowing what he feared. It was no doubt the fear of the unknown.

"What a dream; or, was it just a dream?" Gabe asked himself.

CHAPTER 17

▼

In the Council's Chambers, on this evening, in the Midway Building, voices mingled as dignitaries stood about in a large, white room, with the tables and chairs arranged in a semicircle. Brown mahogany gleamed as the fluorescent lights in the ceiling flickered now and then.

"It's seven-thirty, gentlemen," said Mayor Horace Bowles, a fat old white gentleman, with gray eyes, and neatly trimmed gray hair, wearing a two-piece gray wool suit, a navy-blue shirt, a red-and-black striped tie, and black wingtip shoes. His joviality just sort of bubbled up out of him the many times he smiled or chuckled.

Mayor Bowles slammed the gavel on the podium that he stood behind, one, two, three, and four times, louder and louder, to get everyone's attention. "Please, be seated gentlemen in the seat with your name in front of it on the designated table. We have to get this show on the road," he said, and everyone chuckled at the saying.

He looked a little anxious as the men seemed too slow to get themselves seated. After a couple more slams of the gavel, everyone was finally seated. Still the red-flush on Mayor Bowles' jowls meant that he was less than patient with Council-members.

As usual, the noise in the City Council's Chambers came to a hushed silence. Mayor Bowles addressed those thus assembled:

"Distinguished colleagues, councilmen, law officials and other dignitaries, we've called this meeting this evening to discuss a sanguine problem existing in our downtown area," he said, sounding like Edward R. "Murray," a well-known radio commentator. "We will listen to two gentlemen this evening, after which, we will ask your opinions on how we are to proceed to best remedy the existing problem at hand," he said. A few mumbles around the room caused the Mayor to slam his gavel down hard a couple more times to restore quietness.

"Order! Order!" bellowed Mayor Bowles. "Let us hear from Doctor Whims."

Mayor Bowles beckoned to a gentleman in the audience. He stated with pride, "To some let me introduce, and to others, let me present, Dr. Grover McHarry Whims, President of the University of Virginia. He's here to address the Council on matters of the utmost importance. What goes on downtown affects the University just as much as it does us. Come on up, Dr. Whims, we are glad you could come."

Applause rang out like a bell as a distinguished-looking man with dark-brown hair, graying around the edges, stood up from the middle table of the semicircle. He wore a dark-blue suit, brown penny loafers, a light-blue shirt with a red-and-blue striped tie, on a six-foot athletic-frame. He held a written speech in his left hand.

Some Councilmen groaned, eliciting a few raps of the Mayor's gavel.

Dr. Whims plopped the written speech down on the podium, straighten out his tie, and cleared his throat. He had his hands clasped behind him. He leaned over the podium, and you could hear a pin drop in the Council's Chambers.

"Greetings to Mayor Bowles, and distinguished Councilmen," he said, then he looked around the Chambers making eye contact with each one.

"I feel it is essential that I address the Council on the matter up before it this evening. The city of Charlottesville and the University are just one great big old community," said Dr. Whims, then he got a sip of water from a cup he took from under the shelves of the podium. He straighten his tie a little again.

"Gentlemen, I know that you are aware that our 'Niggras' are running amok all over this city and our country. Right now, even as I speak, and as you all well know, in Georgia and Alabama, a Black rascal called Martin King is leading a communist movement against the constitutional laws of our country, and especially against the laws protecting the South against racial outrage.

"We have a liberal Catholic heading our government in the White House and, bleeding-heart liberal Jews have taken over Congress. Political morals across the country are sinking fast …"

Each Councilman clapped loudly. Dr. Whims pulled out a white silk handkerchief to wipe the sweat off his brow. His confidence was embolden.

"Don't misunderstand me gentlemen, I don't have anything against our good, local, 'Niggras.' Some of them clean my classrooms better than anyone else could. I don't know what we'd do without them, to tell the truth. I've got a darling little maid, that my family and I are greatly depended on, as well as our gardener and our cook at home. You see," Dr. Whims paused for a minute to look around the Chambers. "We all have a need for good 'Niggras' in their rightful place," he said, to even louder applause.

Some Councilmen shouted, "Here-here!"

"It's them troublemaking 'Niggras' we got to be concerned with. They want to integrate our good white-schools! They want to rape our young ladies! They want to assault our young gentlemen! They want to beat white men to death! These are threatening our great white civilization bequeathed to us by our God-fearing founding fathers. We will have a tremendous battle on our hands, if we are going to be able to pass on to the next generation the superior intellectual, moral and social attainments and scientific and economic development, that have catapulted us into the leadership of the world. That is what is at stake, gentlemen.

"Every God-fearing white man in America is obligated to act swiftly, decisively, and immediately for the sake of everything that we all hold dearly, to stop the awful Black-blight now overwhelming our downtown area. A 'Niggra' presence down here is most counterproductive. We must act forthwith to remove them out of that Vinegar Hill slum right away! I tell you ..." Thunderous applause and aggressive feet-stomping interrupted Dr. Whims. The Mayor stood and waved his hand, holding the gavel, with a twisted, little, smile on his face, but he did not rap with it.

"We will get rid of the slummy conditions, when we get rid of the people responsible for creating them. Gentlemen, I mean to say without equivocation or doubt, we must exterminate Vinegar Hill like we would a rat-infested house! I say, let the slum come crumbling down! We will stop strong-arm robbers, Black rapists, and criminals from coming off that Hill and preying upon our innocent students. The time is at hand.

"Informed sources tell me that a so-called 'Civil Rights Bill' winging its way through Congress will more than likely gain speed and pass; and, our liberal President is going to put his stamp of approval on it. It will turn the South topsy-turvy! What I am trying to instill in your minds is, we will not be able to keep 'Niggras!' out of anything they want to come into then; our homes, our churches, our schools, or our communities. Through our schools, we will witness the complete mongrelization of white civilization in America, if Black children are allowed to freely integrate with our white children in public education. We would soon be torn from the top-tier to the bottom-rung of the world's great civilizations. This is what I believe is in store for us if we do not act fast ..."

Dr. Whims had to pause, for the thunderous applause and stomping of the floor went on for a few moments, without any interruption from Mayor Bowles. The Councilmen grew quieter on their own.

"Up at the University, we had to admit a Black Law Student into our Law School, and we have admitted a couple of Black Nursing Students. We didn't want to be thus obligated, but these are already mature and know their place. They pose no threat to us, whatsoever! But, those 'Niggras!' residing on that Vinegar Hill slum, could become a voting bloc, if the voting rights portion of that Civil Rights Bill becomes law. That would mean, we'd see a dusty face or two on Council. Gentlemen, I hope you will agree with me. We must be committed to the proposition that politically, whites and Blacks here must always remain 'Separate but Equal!'

"Thank you gentlemen. I relinquish the floor to Mayor Bowles," said Dr. Whims. He picked up his speech off the podium, and hearing thunderous applause, and seeing a standing ovation, humbly retired to his previous seat.

Mayor Bowles dashed back up to the podium carrying his gavel. He rapped it several times trying to bring the Councilmen to order. The Chambers echoed the applause outside and for about five minutes or so the cheering and clapping went on.

Dr. Whims stood up, bowed himself humbly, and then graciously reseated himself.

After the noise and applause had quieted down to a late clap or two, Mayor Horace Bowles, all smiles now, rapped with his gavel to achieve absolute quiet if possible, and shouted, "Let's give Dr. Whims another round of applause, gentlemen!"

The Chambers roared like thunder for a few minutes. Dr. Whims stood and bowed himself as before. Then the rapping of the Mayor's gavel got the Councilmen's absolute attention.

"Next, gentlemen, we're going to hear a short speech from our own Detective Clemm Doll. He's one of our most aggressive homicide investigators. Come on up here, Clemm," said Mayor Bowles.

Doll walked slowly, swaggering, looking at the floor, with a nervous frown on his troubled face. He wore a two-piece tan-khaki-suit, a yellow and black striped tie over a white shirt. His brown boots sparkled from being overly polished. He stepped to the podium without a prepared speech.

"I agree with Dr. Whims. We must act fast to get rid of them Black pests in our downtown area. All of them must go! The good ones will eventually breed bad ones, just give them time! When they are gone, then we will be able to clean up our fair city!" said Doll. He got out a styrofoam cup from under the podium, poured a cup of water from a pitcher, and gulped it down, like he might would a cup of liquor. Sweat beaded up on his nose, chin and forehead.

Mayor Bowles pointed to his Rolex Watch. Doll knew to cut his speech even shorter.

"Gentlemen, I tell you all, my heart bleeds for the family of little Stanley Graham Longfellow. They sent that kid up here to get educated. But he got cut down by our unsavory 'Niggras!' Now, that's a doggone shame! I promise you the guilty will pay along with all of their cohorts. This I will guarantee you! Thank y'all for listening," said Doll. He walked away from the podium, seeming to wipe tears from his eyes. Everyone in the Council's Chambers clapped loudly, but not as loud or as long as they had for Dr. Whims. The Chambers got very quiet. Doll wiped his brow with a white handkerchief. Quietness pervaded the Chambers, so much so, that Mayor Bowles did not have to rap with his gavel. Doll made his way back to his seat and sat down.

"The floor is now open for motions, gentlemen. How do you plead?" asked Mayor Bowles. "You know what we're here to do."

A chubby gentleman dressed in a dark-brown suit raised his nubby fingers. His bushy-blond hair shook this way and that as he tried to get the Mayor's attention.

"The Chair recognizes Councilman, Tim Morrison. What is your pleasure, sir?" said Mayor Bowles.

"I motion that we form a committee to do a feasibility study on how to best raze the Vinegar Hill slum to the ground. We can call it 'The Vinegar Hill Renewal Project.' We can use those findings to get rid of all of the other 'Niggra' slums, too. That's all, sir," said Councilman Morrison, his voice sounding like a pig's squeal.

A tall, lanky gentleman, wearing a black suit, white shirt and thin blue bow tie, rose up suddenly and blurted out, "I second the motion." He sort of stumbled a little after speaking. He was drunk as a skunk, and forgot to wait to be recognized.

"I'm sorry, Mr. Brice Lamb. You're out of order. The Chair cannot recognize you," said Mayor Bowles. Lamb ran his hands over his short, crewcut red hair. He frowned. Then he stood up immediately before anyone else had a chance, raising his left hand high. His green eyes were bloodshot and bugged out. "I second the motion," he said, slightly slurring his words as he spoke.

"The Chair has to recognize, Mr. Lamb," allowed Mayor Bowles, reluctantly. He has seconded the motion proposed by Councilman Morrison, all right?" said Mr. Bowles, in very pointed speech. He watched Lamb slump down into his seat.

Mayor Bowles rolled his eyes, then slammed his gavel down. "It has been proposed and seconded that we form an investigative committee to evaluate a feasible way to demolish the Vinegar Hill slum. All in favor raise your hand," all raised their hand except one.

"All opposed, raise your hand," and no one did, although one Arthur Bland Gilbert did not vote either way.

"The motion has been carried by a majority of those present and voting. Anyone dissenting may do so by letter by the end of the month. We will meet next week to form a feasibility committee to study the problem discussed on this evening," said Mayor Bowles. "Next week, gentlemen, bring your lawyers, consultants, and position papers. Let's get moving on this one ASAP. Is there any old business that we need to discuss at this time?" he asked, then he looked all over the Chambers. No one's hand was raised. Then he asked, "Is there any other new business that we need to get on the agenda this evening?" No hands were raised again.

"Council is dismissed," said Mayor Bowles, with a sturdy rap of the gavel. The Chambers emptied except for Clemm Doll.

"Can you stay back for a little while, Horace?" asked a shaky Doll, his dusty face showing great anxiety.

"Yeah, I got a few more minutes to give this-here long meeting, Clemm, I reckon," said Horace Bowles. "What do you want to discuss, now?"

"Horace, listen. We know exactly which one of them Vinegar Hill crowd killed that student up yonder at the University!" said Clemm, with both fists clenched. He twisted up his face into a very angry frown.

"Clemm, old buddy, tell me more. I'm all ears. I'll stay as long as your information rings bells," said Horace, excitedly.

"Well, Horace. It's like this: We beat the living hell out of James Killeen and Bubbles Quayles the other day. I mean we–well–darn-near killed them 'coons. Hey, man. We then put them in a bugged cell while they were still bleeding and sore, so we could listen to them complain. In their complaining, one of them said that Bobcat Hinter, off the Hill, killed that student at the University with his fists," said Clemm.

"Which one of them boys said it, Clemm?" asked Horace.

"It was that high-yellow one, James. He's scared of going to prison," said Clemm. "I think he's scared of ending up in the arms of a convict."

"I've heard of James and Bubbles. But who is this Bobcat Hinter?" asked Horace.

"His real name is George Washington Hinter, Jr." said Clemm.

"That's Tee's and old George's boy. They all live up on the Hill. I didn't know he was called 'Bobcat' though," said the Mayor, with a little wince. "Why is he called by that horrible name?"

"Let me tell you something, Horace!" replied Clemm, almost shouting. "That buck started to squeeze an Ape during a wrestling contest at the State Fair, and the owner had to stop the match because that boy would've killed that animal. That Ape had pooped all over the floor! That boy is a hell of a buck–I must say!" said Clemm. His excitement reached a level resembling a little child at a circus. "Tain't no one or two white men–armed or not–who are going to be able to bring that boy down." A ring of disgust vibrated in Clemm's voice.

"Clemm, you know, back in the day, we used to string bucks like him up in a heartbeat! There's a tree up on East High Street, an old Oak tree, that's where a lot of bad bucks met their fate at the end of a rope. I'm talking about much simpler times, though," said Horace.

"We didn't have to ask them people to do something twice, Clemm. Now, those were the good-old-days. It's the Supreme Court. It has betrayed the South. Now we got to watch what the hell we're doing when we go to handle them," Horace bellowed. "Clemm, we've lost a lot of control over our 'Niggers!'"

"Yeah, I know where you're coming from, Horace. We can't use those good-old-methods no more. It's a darn shame, too. Even though we know that Bobcat boy is guilty as hell, we can't legally arrest him. What we did, Horace, is totally illegal. Would never hold up in court, even though that boy killed a white man. The NAACP would eat us alive," shouted Clemm. "I'd soon cut out that buck's balls and pickle them in a jar if it was left up to me. It's that Dr. Martin Luther King, Jr., he's the jack-daddy of it all! I'd like to be the one to gun that puffed-up 'Nigger' down," shouted Clemm. "He makes getting-even with them people a lot harder than it used to be."

"Clemm, we got to figure out a way around the law to bring justice for that Longfellow student, and his grieving family," said Horace. The watering of his eyes showed his emotions. "Were thousands of people up at that young man's funeral, from all walks of life. Just as many Blacks as whites! His death have done more towards bringing the races together around here than anything King and them ever did. See, that's why his senseless murder was such a travesty!

"We got to do something–and do it fast–I tell you that, Clemm! Charlottesville is getting a bad name. Good white people may start to think we can't control our 'Niggers,' and stop sending their children down here to the University. Now, wouldn't that be the straw to break the camel's back?" said Horace. He anxiously rung his hands, and started to pacing back and forth in the Council's Chambers. "We've got to put them back in their place, Clemm!"

"Surely, Horace. But wait a second. Let me run this by you," said Clemm. Both men stopped in the middle of the floor to face each other. A look of dead-seriousness filled up their fearful faces.

"Horace, I know just how to get that buck, and his high-yellow sidekicks. I know we can kill two birds with one stone—so to speak—and nobody will be the wiser. Won't nobody be able to do a doggone thing!" said Doll, letting some air whistle through his teeth.

"Clemm. Clemm. Old buddy, you got to be more than careful about abusing the Negroes these days; now, I done told you about …"

"Horace, I know … I know! Man, I know how to do this crap, now. When I and the good-old-boys get through, them colored-boys will be a darn good example for the rest of the Hill-Rats, I promise you that," said Doll.

Doll smiled broadly. "Heck, we'll just let Bubbles and James go for lack of evidence. That's what we'll put in the papers and on the radio news. They will brag to their buddies for a couple of days, then they will disappear from the face of the earth, like them 'Black rapists' do down there in Mississippi. That's how we'll let white-Christian-justice prevail," said Doll. "Horace, I believe in 'White Power!'"shouted Clemm.

"Clemm. Clemm, you're talking about some deep do-do. Look. I got to tell you up-front, when push comes to shove, I ain't going to own up to nothing at all. We never had this conversation. Is that clear, buddy?" said Mayor Horace Bowles.

"Yeah, boss, I see where you're coming from," said Clemm, with his eyes downcast.

"All right, then. It's about time to get out of this building, Clemm."

"Yeah, I'm right behind you, sir."

As both of the men walked out into the hallway, Vera Crenshaw came from around a corner carrying two porcelain buckets. They had forgotten that it was time for her to come to work. How much Vera had heard, neither Horace nor Clemm knew. Truth is, she had come to work early that night to get a head start on her cleaning. She had heard most of what had been said. That's how Gabe found out.

CHAPTER 18

▼

Detective Doll left the Council's Chambers that night in a state of high-agitation. He talked to himself when he got like that. "Whenever I got to face the 'Niggra' problem head-on, it screws with my head," he said in hushed tones full anxiety and angst; and as he crossed the parking lot of the Midway Building, he spit out a thick, yellow ball of phlegm that had been collecting in his throat all evening. He allowed, "I wish every 'Nigger' in this country a violent death tonight!" He got to the city-owned blue 1963 Plymouth Sedan he had been assigned and sat down in the driver's seat. He reached under it to retrieve a bottle of J&B Scotch. He unscrewed the top, got a styrofoam cup out of the glove compartment, and poured it full of liquor. He gulped it down all at once, then he poured another and another.

The liquor rushed to Clemm's head, making him somewhat delirious. So, he rambled on: "Great-grandma-Mary-Beth! What ... In! The Hell! ... Ever possessed you? How did you ever get so down that you saddled with a tawny-buck instead of a white man? Oh–God!"

Schizophrenic voices swirled around Clemm's head accompanied by ghostly images. "Einy, Meany, Miny, Mo ... I Know, Your Daddy-Mo ... Was A Negro!" a chorus of little white children taunted at him. Laughing faces, little imps, with very sharp teeth they became. With their mouths closing in, he could see their black hearts beating! All his life, he'd had to listen to that crap!

"Oh, I wish that drop of 'Nigger-Blood' coursing through my veins was a cancer instead. Then, at least I could get it cut out! That Godforsaken drop of Black blood can't be singled out, or measured, and is not readily identifiable! But it's there, condemning me to 'Niggerdom!'" hispered Clemm, in a silent scream.

"Doggone it, I'm white! I'm white, no matter what nobody says. I'm white because I choose to be white, God-Bless-It!" shouted Clemm out loud. He cranked up his car and sped out on Main Street. Soon, he was heading on up 29-North.

Clemm parked in front of a white picket fence on Greenbrier Drive in the Northeast corner of Charlottesville, out in Albemarle County. His brick bungalow was a picture-perfect copy of the neat homes that had been constructed there. Many were still being built.

Staggering across his manicured lawn, Clemm was glad that his Black gardener had done his job well. He was so drunk, he had trouble finding the keyhole.

"There … Got it. Hey, I got it," said Clemm.

The glossy brown door of the bungalow swung open at last. In staggered Clemm. "Polly. Polly," he yelled in a drunken but somewhat agitated state. "Polly Ann, come the hell in here, lady," he ordered.

A slender, beautifully curvaceous blonde in her late twenties or early thirties came into the front room, nervously approaching her inebriated husband. She had on a pink housecoat that came all the way to her ankles. It was sheer enough so that her voluptuous body was visible through it. She, Brenda Crenshaw, and her two girls had been awakened by the noise that Clemm was making.

"Lady, what're you standing there whimpering about? Come on. Come on over here, pull old Clemm's boots off. I'll fall on the darn floor if I try to bend over and do that–you know that. Might fall asleep on the floor and be down here all night long. Now, we don't want me to do that, sugar, now do we?" said Clemm, with a twisted sinister smile going across his drunken face, as he beckoned with his hands. Polly went over to her drunk husband, sprawled out on the floor, as quickly as she dared. Brenda peeps through the door of the girls' bedroom.

"All right, darling. I'll be right there," said Polly in a soft, sweet, nervous voice. She fought back the tears coming to her eyes by incessantly blinking her eyelids. But her bluish-eyes kept filling up and a tear or two escaped.

"I'm hungry as a ravenous wolf, 'gal.' But I know you ain't got nothing on the stove–can't smell a thing cooking," said Doll, with a snarl resembling a dog's.

"Honey, you know I'll be glad to fix anything for you. You know that, anything that you want …"

Polly was knocked across the room into one of her floor lamps, that sat in each corner of her front room. Her pretty head hit the wall. Doll had kicked her.

"Doggone it, Polly," shouted Doll, his speech slurring into a continuous drawl.

"You're a stupid white! … You're acting like poor-white trash or something. Whenever I come home, I want to eat. Five minutes after I get here, I want to smell something good cooking in the kitchen. Now, get your cute little butt in that kitchen and get me some grub ready, directly," shouted Clemm, a familiar rage in his voice made Polly tremble all over.

"I'll fix it right away," she blurted out. "Clemm. Clemm! Don't hit me no more in front of my girls. I don't want that to grow up in them, seeing their mother beaten by their father. You don't have to do that, Clemm!" screamed Polly. She got up off the floor and tried to rush by Clemm to get to the kitchen.

Another lick caught Polly on the side of her face. It raised an ugly whap on her cheeks. She sat down on the floor in a bit of a daze. Doll stood over her preparing to jam his harden fist into his lovely wife's pretty face, again.

"Get up! Get up, 'Bitch!' I'll swell your lips up bigger than a 'Nigger's'"Doll yelled. He staggered around like a wounded enraged animal.

"Clemm, I'm hurt bad. I can taste my blood in my mouth, Clemm. Don't hit me no more … I'm hurt bad…." Polly whined so pitifully. She blacked out.

Brenda and Doll's two blond teenaged girls came running out of a bedroom towards Polly laid out on the floor almost unconscious. One of the girls was shorter than the other. Their green matching nighties flowed as they ran to Polly. Both screamed, "Daddy! Daddy! Don't hit momma again. Stop! Stop! Please stop!"

Polly was dazed and hurting, but managed to get up off the floor. She reached out to her girls, sobbing right along with them.

"Mr. Doll, I know I ain't s'pose to get in y'all's business, but if you lay another hand on Mrs. Polly, I'm going to jail for you. You's a cop, and I s'pects more out of you than that. If you want to hit somebody, try to hit me!" screamed Brenda. She stood with both fists balled up.

"Y'all ganging up on me. That ain't right! This is my house. I am the law. I got a right to protect my home," shouted Clemm. Then he yanked out his snub-nosed Forty-Five. He waved the gun around, at Polly, then Brenda. He looked towards his girls.

The tallest and oldest girl closely resembling her mother screamed hysterically at her drunk father, "I hate you! I hate you! Why do you have to come home drunk and be so mean to us? Go ahead and shoot, daddy–I don't care!"

Brenda, the girls and Polly clung to each other. Then Polly allowed, "Oh, Clemm. Clemm. Clemm! Go ahead and shoot me! But let these go! I'm the one you hate–isn't that right?" she said. Then she pointed at her girls. "Carol," the oldest and "Charlotte," the youngest, "Y'all go on back to bed with Brenda, it's me he wants."

"No!" both Brenda and the girls yelled. "No! No! No!"

"All of you, go into that room, right now!" shouted Polly, pointing at the door of their bedroom. Tears streamed down her lovely cheeks, and all four females sobbed like some lambs bleating. The ten and twelve year old girls cried even louder.

Seeing the women and girls crying and whimpering so, got to Clemm. The J&B was losing some of its potency and common sense revived in his warped mind. "It's them Black rascals that's got me all wound up!" shouted Clemm. He fell to his knees on the floor, whimpering like a little puppy. He looked up at his girls with red, bloodshot eyes, snorting his nose like a bull, and cried out louder.

"Carol Puddin. Char-Char. Polly Ann. I'm … I'm not myself. Them Black rascals bring out the worst in me. I get like this sometimes. I don't know why.…"

"If you don't know what's wrong, Mr. Doll, let me tell you. You's prejudice as hell! You're hateful and mean to us Black folks. One day you will get yours from the Man Up Above, though. Just you wait and see!" screamed Brenda.

"Come on Brenda. Let me take you home. You can see that Clemm is not in any shape to drive you. Wrap up the girls and bring them along. Let's leave this drunk on the floor where he's balled up and sleeping it off. Let's go," said Polly.

"Einy, meany, miny, mo, I know your daddy-mo was a Negro! … " The words haunted Clemm's inner-being, his dreams, his every thought. They corrupted his soul. Turned him in on himself. Too black to be white and too white to be black, that's what they meant. They were a closet-secret, that was like a hot fire burning in his mind, devouring up his sanity and reason. *Least that's what he thought!*

CHAPTER 19

▼

Gabe couldn't stand working at the UVA any longer. He got a job at a place up 250 West. It was where all of the white muck'ta'muck of high-society hung out. Being a busboy up there was a step up for Gabe. Well, it was better than scrubbing walls, taking out trash, and waxing floors, or was it? Although Gabe knew that there was nothing wrong with janitorial work to make an honest living, he figured that a young intelligent Afro-American should not restrict himself to just that menial occupation. And, furthermore, Gabe wanted to get away from having to face old George all day.

Mayor Bowles, Dr. Whims, and Antonio DiCappio belonged to the Antebellum Inn Country Club, they were lifelong members. DiCappio's membership surprised Gabe. He was a Northerner. He did not descend from any of the old Southern families, a prime qualification for membership consideration. On this evening in September, 1963, Mayor Bowles, at taxpayers' expense, sponsored an elegant banquet to which most Charlottesville-Albemarle officials–the upper-crust–were invited. On their invitations–in rather tiny red-print–were "We are going to discuss the finer points of the Negro Problem."

Gabe and his Black co-workers had set up the Crystal Room of the Inn. The Inn, a one-story brick edifice architecturally resembling the buildings of ancient Greece, had huge white columns, and green marble steps leading up to its elegant stained-oak doors, with carved ivory handles. Out in back of the Inn, a multitude of beautiful flowers darted the landscape. Trees with red leaves, blue leaves and purple leaves accented the carpeted lawns making for an exquisite floral and shrubbery display on grounds, that could be clearly seen through the many ceiling-to-floor windows and similar doors on the back-end and all around the Inn.

Gabe watched the group gathering in the Crystal Room as fancy-gowned women and men wearing dinner tuxedos strode past Mayor Bowles, who was similarly attired. Mr. Bowles looked all around at the Crystal Room with its glowing walls of white marble that accentuated the light, making a huge chandelier in the middle of the ceiling seem to glow like the sun. It's candelabra were like sparkling stars. Its base was of gold with silver tentacles and pearl beads dangling around the base of it.

"We are directly descended from God. This room makes me realize that more than anywhere else in Charlottesville. I believe we were meant to rule over all of mankind even as we are doing. God put us here to be the rulers of this world, and any other race trying to usurp that authority is out of God's will," said Mayor Bowles to Mr. and Mrs. Doll as they strolled into the Crystal Room. Mr. Doll got a little twisted smile on his dark-complexioned face, but Mrs. Doll got a grimace on hers.

I hope God was not as pale as this bloated woodpecker is, and I hope direct descendants of God would be a lot different than any of these people for God-Sake! thought Gabe. *But I believe this Mayor Bowles believes what he's saying way down in his racist soul. He probably doesn't even know that it's just that old "Segregation Crap!"*

Mayor Bowles strutted across the cream-colored tile on the floor like he was Julius Caesar or Mark Anthony. He smiled from arrogant ear-to-arrogant ear. The Crystal Room filled up with various dignitaries that seated themselves around end to end banquet tables with mirror tops that had crystal-like designs etched in them. Mr. Bowles seated himself in an antique-looking chair covered with red cashmere, as were the rest of the chairs at the tables, that seemed to be Tudor-styled and of white mahogany, resting on golden loin-claws.

Bowles stood up at an end table after the crowd had moseyed in and got seated. He smiled and began speaking: "Good evening ladies and gentlemen. I can't help but feel really regal today," he said. The crowd applauded those remarks with gusto. He went on, "A noble descendant of our European ancestors is about to address us. We would do well to listen to every word he has to say," said Mr. Bowles. He looked around the room at those seated. "First, let me recognize Chief of Police, Lennie Moon and his lovely wife, Carla; our three fine Councilmen, Lamb, Morrison, and Arthur Gilbert and their fine wives, Logan, Brenda and Cecilia; City Manager, Cooley Mason; and Mr. and Mrs. Doll; and last, but not least, Mr. and Mrs. Whims. We are proud to have all of you here at this banquet and symposium this evening. Before we hear from our guest speaker, we will be served," he said. "Here comes the food now," said Mayor Bowles, pointing at a group of Black servers wearing white, busboy, crow-tailed, coats, black trousers, patent leather shoes, white, ruffled-shirts, with tiny bow ties, pushing several serving carts loaded with cuisine. Bowles sat down as the male servers came into the Crystal Room's hallway.

Cheese, cracker and vegetable trays were on the first carts, along with various fine wines, champagne, and bottles of ale and beer. Three Black women wearing black busgirl dresses with white aprons, and little white bonnets perched on top of their heads, got busy distributing the Inn's place mats, that had the Confederate Bars and Stars logo, that was also on the cloth napkins. The plates, bowls, assorted dishes and the handles of the silverware had the same logo imprinted on or carved on them. The cheese, crackers and vegetables were soon gone, as were all of the beverages.

Another group of Black servers came in with other carts loaded with steaming hot Prime Rib of Beef, Crown Roast; Leg of Lamb; Broiled Snapper; and Stuffed Flounder with shrimp, lobster and watercress stuffing; and, a fresh-steamed vegetable-medley was served off of a variety of silver platters, or out of silver bowls. Then later a third group came with about ten varieties of cakes and pies seemingly of every flavor imaginable. Finally, a decorative fried ice cream dish rounded out the desserts. Tea and or coffee was served to top off the splendid banquet.

The tables were orderly cleared of dishes, replaced by bright-colored place mats that depicted various Civil War scenes. Gabe noticed that Tony DiCappio was a little annoyed at the place mats, just judging by the sneer on his face. Without waiting to be properly announced, Tony came up to the podium all at once. He tapped on the edge of the podium and as the servers melted away, he spoke up:

"Hello, everybody. I'm Tony DiCappio," said the muscular mob guy.

"Hello, Tony," the audience answered back. Then a hush came over the place.

"I have had a talk with Dr. Whims, City Manager Mason, youse local law officials, and I have here in my hand a plan that will work for youse city if youse choose to elect it. I am partnered with a construction firm out of New Jersey, 'Valentino, Serpentino, and Luciano.' We're into the demolition of slummy housing and buildings and feel that our firm could be of a lot of service to youse good people to help youse solve your immediate problems with the 'jiggerboos.'

"If youse would work with me and my company, you'd be rid of that slum in youse downtown area in no time at all. We got the equipment, and we're ready to go at the most reasonable prices. The City Manager has copies of our proposal and bid, and I want that youse should go look these over and vote to hire my firm," said Tony. "Thank youse all for your time."

A few people in the audience clapped loudly, but stopped when they saw no great outpouring of applause. But Dr. Whims jumped up. "The man has my support," he said. He looked around at familiar faces.

"Has mine, too," said Councilman, Morrison.

"Here-here," said Councilman, Lamb.

"I enjoyed the speech by Mr. DiCappio," said Mayor Bowles. "I'm willing to give Mr. DiCappio any aid he might need or require to get rid of that slum downtown. We have decided that we have our demolition firm. The job is about to commence. The renewal of that slummy area is about to begin."

The Black-male servers had returned with trays bearing Scotch, Vodka, Gin, Bourbon, Rum, and Sour Match liquors. All were very expensive, St. George, Hennessy, Johnny Walker, etc. The servers went around to all of the guests in the Crystal Room. Most of them took a sparkling crystal glass with two ice cubes in it. The servers poured liquor into their glasses. After each glass had been filled, Mayor Bowles said:

"Let me propose a toast," he chimed. All of the guests raised their glasses. "Here's to the end of one era, and the beginning a new one. May we all prosper and reap lucrative rewards in the very near future." He gulped his glass of Scotch right down the hatch. All of the guests followed through. It was finished.

Several of the guests got up and headed to the hallway to get their coats and hats. A few lingered to partake of the alcohol. Doll and Mayor Bowles downed glass after glass. They were flanked by Councilmen, Lamb, Morrison, and Gilbert.

Soon the Crystal Room was emptied of its guests. Gabe felt like crying. *These people are going to destroy a way of life for over a hundred innocent people because of the errant actions of one or two. It has to be more to it than that. They got to know that nine-out-of-ten of the people living on Vinegar Hill's 20-acre-tract, are law-abiding citizens. They are not killers, robbers, or rapists. They work in these peoples' homes, at their businesses, and at City Hall. They are not condemning the Hill for fear of crime—nobody will ever be able to convince me of that,* thought Gabe. As Gabe helped clean up the Crystal Room, suddenly the whiteness of the place made him feel sick to his stomach. He ran to the "Colored Employees' restroom," and threw up.

CHAPTER 20

▼

Gabe needed some fresh air. He stepped outside in time to hear: "Polly, Polly. Come back here. Where you going!" shouted Doll to his distraught wife. She turned, stood still, her eyes becoming aqua-marine in color, being filled with tears, that messed up her mascara. She started hysterically yelling at her husband, who tried to grab her and pull her to him. She broke away from him. She looked up into his face, her body trembling all over as she almost screamed.

"Clemm, they're talking about the complete removal of a lot of good ol' 'colored people.' People who haven't done nothing to be shoved off the face of the earth like you and those rich, fat-cats in city government are planning to do! I will have no part in this crappy deal, Clemm!" screamed Polly loudly, not seeming to care who heard her.

Doll put his hand over her mouth for a second. "Hush, baby. Somebody will hear you. We don't want them to think we're backing out," hissed Doll through clenched teeth.

"I have never been in favor of any plan you crooks downtown came up with when it comes to abusing our nice 'Negroes!' Clemmon Doll," came out of the side of Polly's lips. She paced back and forth in front of Doll, wringing her hands.

"You go on, Clemm," she exclaimed. "I'm not riding in that car with you. You're too drunk to drive. Now, I wish you and all of your bosom-buddies would get the hell out of my face for good!" screamed Polly. Some of the guests started over to the red-carpet leading into the entrance of the Antebellum Inn, but Doll waved his hand to let them know everything was under control.

"Polly, Polly, look. Look, honey. Let's go home and talk about this, not out here in public like this … Okay?"

"Why? … So you can beat the hell out of me some more, Clemm!" yelled Polly.

"All right, then. Go on. Get home the best way you can, I don't care!" hissed Doll. He gave his parking-card to a white valet. "Bring my car around to the curb. I'm getting the hell out of 'Dodge City,'"said Clemm. Then he whispered to himself–but Gabe heard–"Should've left that little white-trash up yonder in Sugar Hollow where I met her, doggone her!" Doll's car came right after that, and he quickly sped away.

"Got to warn … somebody. Got to tell somebody. People going to suffer. Somebody got to stop this madness …" whined Polly. She looked towards Gabe remembering his facial features from the bus station.

"Will you call me a cab, sir?" she asked Gabe.

That was one of a few times a white person in Charlottesville had ever said "sir," or anything like that to him. So Gabe was shocked. "Yes ma'am," he said.

In about fifteen minutes, a Yellow Cab came to pick up Polly. She got into the backseat of the Cab and allowed, "To 2020 Greenbrier Drive, please."

"This is a mistake, ma'am. I thought … Well, only the colored help usually call for a cab out here. So they sent me thinking that you's … I hope some white man is go ride along with us. We got to be safe for both our sakes, ma'am. You know what I'm saying?" said the fat jovial-looking, deep-ebony, driver.

"Listen to me! I'm sick and tired of all of this color-stuff! There isn't any white man coming to ride with me. Now, start this cab up and take me home, sir. Right now!" screamed Polly.

"Yes'am. Yes ma'am," said the driver. His voice trembled as he spit out the words he uttered. Polly hated yelling at him like that, but she felt that this crap has got to stop, and that's all to it. The driver started up the car and they were off. Polly wept silently most of the way home. Then she prayed, "God, help us all.…"

CHAPTER 21

▼

On September 20, 1963, Bubbles and James could not believe their ears.

"Evening Boys," went Doll. "Y'all boys are lucky as hell. We can't hold you no longer. Lack of evidence is what the problem is. We got to turn you loose. Y'all's free to go," said Doll. He inserted the key into the electric lock, and the cell door slammed open.

"Hey James, we're go be free!" said Bubbles. He whispered, "I told you all you had to do was be quiet and everything would be groovy, see?"

"Right-on, my-man," said James. He was anxious as a child is at Christmas.

"I'm going right home and clean up, man. I know grandma will be glad to see me. I don't know why they didn't even allow us one phone call," whined James.

"Let's talk about this later. Ol' Doll got our belongings we came in here with. After I get those, I'm out of here," said Bubbles.

"Bubbles, there's just one thing that bothers me."

"What's that, James?"

"Man. Bubbles. I ain't never heard of nobody getting released at night."

"Don't make no difference nohow, James. Long's we get to walk, that's all that counts, homes. Can't wait to see that Bobcat, man. I got a few things to get off my chest. Way I see it, we can't be walk-partners no more with him!" said Bubbles.

"Yeah–and I want a piece of that Gabe 'G-Man,' too. I bet he's the one who got us fingered in the first place! Here comes Doll. Let's get the hell on out of here," said James.

Doll led Bubbles and James off towards a backdoor of the Jail, used to load and unload murderers when they are considered extremely dangerous. Doll and them had to walk down a narrow hallway to some back steps that led into a basement to the backdoor. Doll unlocked the nine or ten locks on the bars of that door and a final electric lock and it opened and James and Bubbles walked off into the night. Doll did a mocking salute to them as they scampered away, the both of them feeling a little suspicious of Doll's actions.

"This seems too good to be true!" said James.

"Yeah–I know–but let's get the hell out of here, quick, fast, and in a hurry, man," said Bubbles. They split up and ran in different directions....

"Hello. Is this Rosa Killeen?" a husky voice asked on the other end of the telephone call.

"Yes tis," answered Rosa. "You's a white man calling me this early. What you wants?" She was still a little drowsy, and she smacked her lips as she spoke.

"I'm Chief of Police, Lennie Moon. We need you to come down to the station soon as you can, Rosa," said the cold-hearted sounding white-man's voice.

Rosa got dressed in a hurry. Maybe, she'd find out what had happened ... Not a word ... No phone calls ... Those white devils....

Rosa made her way to the station, with her eyes looking like the blazing embers of a coal-fire. She saw the wicked-looking Chief Moon standing at the counter staring at her like a ravenous wolf. She wondered, what, now?

"Come on round the counter with me, Rosa. We got to take you down the hall a' ways," said Chief Moon. He had a cold distant look on his otherwise steely face. Rosa's heart pounded like the rolling thunder. She knew something terrible was about to unfold. "Oh God, help us!" she prayed.

Down the dark hallway, Doll joined them. Rosa Killeen, a fat five-foot lady, with reddish-brown hair, and grayish-green eyes, staggered along now, expecting the worst. "What have y'all done with my grandchild? ... What? ..." she blurted out.

A black door with the big-red letters, "MORGUE," on it, took all the strength out of Rosa. She went limp. Her white Missionary Dress came up her old legs as she slid down to the floor. Moon and Doll had a hard time trying to keep her on her feet.

"What have you ungodly people done to my James?" screamed Rosa out of tight lips drawn together from years of questioning the system.

"Just step this way," said Doll. He pointed to the "MORGUE."

Rosa's legs got real wobbly. She screamed, "You done killed him! You done killed him! Y'all ain't nothing but a bunch of killers!" They all entered the

MORGUE. Doll and Moon jumped back away from Rosa as she yelled, "I'm go puke. I'm go throw up." She gagged, but nothing came up.

Then Moon went over to one of the metal drawers in the MORGUE, snatched it open, and allowed, "Is this your James?"

"Oh God! He's beat to death! Swollen up all over! Y'all done cut his manhood off. Who the hell did this?" screamed Rosa, at the ashen-blue appearance of the corpse of her once handsome grandson.

The world made no sense to Rosa anymore. It swirled out of control, turning into indistinguishable colors that faded into gray then black. Her big eyes rolled back up into her head. Only the whites of them could be seen. She became rigid in the arms of Doll and Moon. Her breath came gushing out of her nose and mouth. Moon and Doll had to just let her down to the floor. A forensic examiner came out and gave Rosa smelling salt, but she could not be revived. "She's gone," he said.

Gabe was getting ready to go to the evening shift out to the Inn when he heard the news on WINN: "Rival ruffians are believed to be the culprits in the gruesome beating of James Killeen, that resulted in his death. Police have no concrete leads at this time. His grandmother, Rosa, passed away at the police station after hearing the news that her grandson had been a victim of murder. More news at seven...."

When Gabe would walk past the corners of Ninth and East High Streets, just around the curve from the Virginia Employment Commission building, he'd be awed by the massive Black Oak tree that stood on that corner. It looked to be about one-hundred-feet in circumference. The years had seen termites hull out its middle, like it was rotting from the soul of it outwards. The wind would blow through the hollowness of its dead and dying limbs, and it would moan like dying men. Gabe had heard that, "hundreds of slaves were hanged on that tree. Then, the wind used to howl through its limbs after each hanging." Now, the old tree was barely alive, being held up by a number of cables, and was patched here and there with what appeared to be asphalt. It was ghastly to behold.

On this morning, the phone rang at police headquarters. "Hello, yes. This is Officer Doll. Calm down. I can't understand a word that you're screaming," Doll hollered into the receiver.

"Detective Doll. Please! Please, come over here quickly," the shrill hysterical voice of a female screamed back at Clemm.

"Ma'am, what's wrong–what's the matter?" yelled Doll right back.

"Sir, I can't believe what's hanging up there on the 'Hanging Tree' out here on High Street!" was the female's comeback.

"What do you see, lady?" asked Doll.

"I want you to come see for yourself! I can't believe we're still seeing this sort of thing in this day and age. No ... No, this just can't be happening," said the excited woman. "You got to come see!"

"Well, ma'am, what's your name, first of all?" asked Doll. The phone "clicked," as the woman dropped the receiver down.

Doll turned to his dispatcher. "Maggie, get on the intercom. Signal Code-187 for Ninth and East High Streets. We're going to need lots of backup, because commuters will be all around the area gawking ..." Doll stopped short of telling the dispatcher what he knew to be up there on East High.

Moon and Doll arrived on the scene early that morning. Officers, Gillen and Pace arrived soon after them. The cops pushed their way through all of the people and commotion up on East High. There were radio news crews, Channels, 29,3, and 12 television crews, and a Black man from the only Black newspaper in town, interviewing people and getting this fantastic occurrence recorded, as the cops made their way to the epicenter of the horrible spectacle.

There was Bubbles just as he had been left, probably very early that morning, or late that night, before the sun came up to reveal the horrid evidence of the dark deeds of hateful men, left hanging on the ol' "Hanging Tree."

A beautiful blonde screamed hysterically, "We thought this kind of thing was over with!" A red-head screamed also, "Doggone murderers! Stupid racists! Whoever done this killing ought to be fried in the electric chair. We need to lynch them!" Other white women were screaming and pumping their fists in the air.

Doll got out a bullhorn. "Y'all break it up!" he ordered. "Let the police do their jobs. Move on, now," shouted Doll. His voice was no more than a duck's quack being drown out by the boisterous crowd. The crowd grew louder and louder.

Moon got on his CB and called for more backup. Soon thereafter, several police cars sped to the scene with their lights flashing and sirens blasting. The cops had on full riot-gear. They got all around the crowd of shouting white people, some carrying broad shields, and some had long batons and others had electric cattle-prods. The cops lit into the crowd meaning to disperse it. A few Black people had stopped by to see what the protest was all about. These were beaten, shocked with the cattle-prods, and arrested for "Disturbing The Peace!" The whites started to leave the scene, still chanting hysterically. Bubbles Quayles' mutilated naked body hanging from that tree was more than the average white person in and around Charlottesville was able to accept. The yelling, screaming crowd made it's way to downtown....

Gabe was nervous as could be. James was dead. Some of the homies blamed for his death. It didn't seem right to Gabe. Who would have the nerve to step to one of the most feared walk-partners? Gabe had no idea who that might be.

"Gabe, go-head-on, cut her on. See what's on the news," said old George. Gabe answered, "All right, Mr. Hinter." He went into the front room, turned a little black button and on came a black and white picture. He clicked the large dial on the side of the twenty-one inch screen of the RCA TV set to local Channel 29.

"This is Channel 29 News. At a little after Six-Thirty, this morning, the police found a local tough-man, called 'Bubbles,' dangling from the fabled 'Hanging Tree,' on East High Street. The actual name of the victim is Leroy Quayles. Homicide investigator, Detective Clemmon Doll says, 'Bubbles probably hanged himself, most likely over the remorse he must've felt for some of the crimes he and his hoodlum friends have committed in the city of Charlottesville and Albemarle County.'"

The newsman's image faded. A large group of shouting white women on East Main Street flashed across the screen. "We Want This To Stop!" they shouted. A slim lady wearing a two-piece gray suit stood on some kind of platform and started addressing the crowd: "Ladies, what do we want?" The crowd answered, "Justice!" The speaker screamed, "When do we want it?" and the crowd answered, "Now!"

The anchorman came back on the screen. "Such is the scene in the downtown area," he said. "Now a word from our sponsors...." Gabe jumped up and ran out of the front room. Up the street he ran. *How long before somebody comes for me? I got to be next. Strange though. Why is it that nobody's arrested Bobcat?* thought Gabe. *Both Bubbles and James are dead–murdered. Did Bobcat do them?*

CHAPTER 22

▼

On this evening, Gabe was off and turned the TV on to get the evening news. A grave-looking news anchorman, Walter Cronkite, came on the screen. He was fighting back the tears as he spoke. "Today, at noon, in Dallas, Texas, President John Fitzgerald Kennedy was shot by a lone gunman from the window of a book depository building, ..." shocked Gabe, Tee, and old George to silence.

Tee dropped down to her knees and so did old George.

"Oh God," Tee prayed. "What's happening? What is our world becoming? Help us God!" She was interrupted by the sound of people yelling and footsteps trampling through the Hill, at laughing young voices, and hurled bricks and bottles crashing into buildings. They all seemed to be heading to the downtown area. Tee could see the edges of downtown from her front windows. A vacant building on the edge of Vinegar Hill was engulfed in flames. "This November 22, 1963 is hell," said Tee. Gabe stood with his mouth wide open. *The pains of being in a hated race, and part of a dreaded subculture had erupted like a volcano, its lava spilling back upon itself. Its ashes blackening out all reason in the minds of oppressed Black people in Charlottesville–and all over America,* was how Gabe saw things.

Nonviolent protests gave way to groups of Black youths venting their frustrations on innocent white store owners, and stores in general. Gangs of swarming young African-Americans came up out of Vinegar Hill, joined by some from other communities in and around Charlottesville, in search of some place to loot and set things straight. Mayor Bowles called in the National Guard, something that had seldom been done. White and Black people of "good will" formed coalitions.

Dr. John Bower, the Pastor of Zion Union Baptist Church, went down Commerce to Second Street, with Sophia Quayles, Chair-person of the Missionary Board, marching with a peace-seeking group of "Love Thy Enemy," demonstrators. They chanted, "Love, Not Hate Is The Way! Peace! Understanding! Forgiveness! Is God's Way!" The mixed-race group held hands and marched down Main Street.

Tee uttered to Gabe, "Son, I see solemn faces, drawn, desolate-looking, with dark circles around their eyes. They don't look optimistic at all, yet they are chanting, "We Shall Overcome!" Tears came down Tee's cheeks. "Those few white marchers among them are not enough to really cause the kind of change they're marching for and chanting about. It's just going to make the gathering white mobs angrier. I wish we'd all let things cool off. We Blacks, we're going to end up getting the worst out of all of this," she harped. "What is America coming to?"

Channel 6 News showed the angry white mobs raining beer bottles, trash, uneaten food, and unfinished sodas on the marchers, as the days went by and the peaceful protestors would not stop marching and chanting. On this evening a group of marchers stopped, kneeled and began to pray at the bottom of Commerce Street, just at the downtown borderline. A UVA professor, Dr. Peter Gladstone, stood while they prayed. He seemed like a watchman, looking this way and that, as angry white youths chanted, "Nigger-Lovers! Race Traders! ..." at the peace-seekers.

An angry white man ran up out of the mob and slammed a brick up beside Dr. Gladstone's head, knocking him to the ground. Blood dripped from the blond professor's head down his cream-colored face. His blond, bushy eyebrows became red as he wiped his hand across his face. His horn-rimmed glasses landed on the sidewalk. His light-blue Summer-suit, showed many, little blood-splatters. He groaned in pain, lying upon the ground, dazed and crying. The vicious youth screamed, "Up-you! You Commie Son of Baal! You humping commie-pinko, egg-sucking, 'Nigger-Lover!' I'll kill you the next time I see you out here cavorting with our good 'Niggras' stirring them up against good white folks!" Then the police arrived. The very aggressive young man's bushy, brown hair got muffled, his T-shirt became stained with his own blood after the cops mauled him, kicked and stomped him. The mob did not disperse. But the cops arrested all of the peaceful demonstrators, "for their own protection," they said. The National Guard surrounded the downtown area. Guns at the ready, bayonets fixed, with murder in their eyes, they brought all activities to an end that evening."I can't stand watching this much longer," said Tee, weeping like someone had died. She turned the channel.

From channel to channel, worse things happened in cities like Washington, D.C., Detroit, Oakland, Los Angeles, Philadelphia and New York. Hordes of Blacks and other people had a looting free-for-all. Social unrest was the order of the day—or the lack of it. This was too depressing to Tee. "I just won't watch this television until all this mess comes to a head," said Tee to Gabe.

After a few days, Vinegar Hill looked like a bomb had been dropped on it. Gabe saw charred remains of some of the already falling down buildings all around the Hill. *Why the hell do Black people get mad and burn down their own neighborhoods? This crap doesn't make no darn sense. My people ... My people, we got a long way to go!* thought Gabe.

C H A P T E R   2 3

▼

The peace marching, and social unrest quieted down after President Lyndon B. Johnson announced on national television that, "I assure you the Civil Rights Bills now before Congress are certain to pass and relieve a lot of the suffering causing people to riot in the poorer Black regions of America. They will be able to buy into the political process with their voting rights protected through tough new legislation, and racial discrimination will be prohibited in all public conveyances by law. All we are asking for is a little more patience and the nightmare of a racially segregated society in America will be over...."

Gabe knew what had prompted that response, though. *Dr. King, James Baldwin, Jesse Jackson, Andy Young, and many others had met with a Blue Ribbon Committee to discuss ways to defuse the rioting in Washington, D.C., in California, South Side, Chicago, North Philadelphia, Richmond, Virginia, and, etc. A Civil Rights Bill was proposed and agreed upon; along with a Voting Rights Act; and Federal Registrars promised for all of the southern states to get rid of unusual tests, poll taxes, and other devious means to keep Blacks from voting.*

But the real reason that Johnson was moved to push Black Civil Rights legislation through Congress, using all of the might of his Democratic Party's political machine was a news flash, that showed black smoke billowing up from smoldering debris where fourteen city-blocks had been leveled by rioting Black youths throwing gasoline Molotov Cocktails, within sight of the White House.

Black Americans were being called upon to fight to preserve democracy in Southeast Asia, when Blacks in America were "Burning, Baby, Burn!" because they felt cast aside and out of the American political processes. The world looked scornfully at America, and nations weighed the prospect of whether to join America in the Vietnam

Conflict or not if it refused to recognize Black Americans as Full-Citizens. Gabe knew this was really what was behind Johnson's, a racist southerner, struggle to push through legislation giving African-Americans the rights that had been previously promised to them via the 13th, 14th, and 15th Amendments to the Constitution; but, had been denied to them through 200-years of States Rights and Introspection in the South, and just plain long old *defacto segregation* in the North.

Gabe reflected on some of the facts he felt he dared not forget: *James and Bubbles died strangely. I don't believe that the homies killed James, and I know Bubbles didn't hang himself. Brothers don't kill themselves. What came over the radio, television, and in the newspapers is just wrong. That's what they want us Blacks to believe. I would swear that the cops killed them walk-partners. What I don't understand is, why is Bobcat still walking around without seeming to have a care in this world?* thought Gabe.

On this particular day, Gabe was off from work. He didn't have to see old George anymore. Changed jobs. Bobcat was never home these days. He roamed alone. He was his same old kick-butt self.

What the hell, Gabe figured he'd bop on down on the Hill, see what's happening. He was thinking that he'd checkout Taylor's Pool Hall. Cop a bottle of beer or two and what not, maybe pick up one of the pretty honeys that came through there. Maybe, Brenda Crenshaw might happen by–he hadn't seen her in a while.

Once inside of Taylor's, Gabe saw the usual crowd of hustlers. Just as he came in that area of Taylor's, Bobcat sank the eight-ball in the corner pocket to beat a poor, country, sucker out of his two-dollars. "Lucky skunk," said the dude, with a sigh.

Bobcat's cold hawk-eyes burned right through Gabe's chest when he spied him standing near the door of the restaurant area, that was more like a counter in the pool hall. Gabe didn't know whether to run or stay. But he got the courage to stay.

"A Change Go Come...." blasted on the jukebox as Big-Red from D.C., bounced into the pool hall, wearing his usual sucker-baiting outfit, flanked by two dudes dressed just like him.

"That jive mo-joe," hissed Bobcat under his breath. "He shucked me last time we played–but I bet he won't do it today," said Bobcat to some walk-partner Gabe had never seen before. "I'm a get his red-bone butt today–been practicing for that since the last time."

"Next!" yelled Big-Red, looking directly into Bobcat's anxious eyes.

"You got it, my-man," said Bobcat. "I'm go fade you like a natural man. Got a bankroll in my pocket just for you, dude. What's happening, now?"

"Bo, go out to the car and get my new stick out of the trunk. We going to be into it, now," said Big-Red to a tall, muscular dude dressed just like him.

When the dude came back, Bobcat allowed, "Red, let's shoot for some real money. One game, for two-hundred-dollars. Let's go for it all. Let's do that eight-ball thing. You the man! You got the bad stick! Can you fade me?"

"Got you covered, homes," said Big-Red.

Jake came in and racked the balls.

"Bobcat, you go on break the balls. Don't miss a shot, my-man. It'll be all over for you. I'm good!" bragged Big-Red.

Ty Smith and one of his walk-partners bopped into the pool hall. They got a table and started shooting pool, laughing softly to themselves, eyeing Bobcat's every move. Gabe could see that they were not very interested in shooting pool.

"You brung your piece, Worm, okay?" whispered Ty to his short walk-partner. "I got mine. Bobcat and them b'lieves in they fists, but this is a new day. We go even the score today. I'm glad Mr. DiCappio hooked us up. This is the best chance we go ever have, Worm."

"I'm digging where you coming from. What did the man drop on you? I got a Thirty-Eight, Snub-nosed? Is that big enough to bring that dude down?" said Worm.

"Don't worry, Worm. I got a Forty-Five-Auto. It shoots hollow points. That'll bring his big butt down," hissed Ty.

After Bobcat broke the balls, the Ten-Ball fell in a corner pocket. "I got the big-balls," shouted Bobcat. He ran all of the balls off the table, slowly but surely. All the hustlers in the pool hall stopped what they were doing and gathered around Bobcat's and Big-Red's table. They were shooting for a lot of money, and everyone wanted to see who'd win. Nobody had beaten Big-Red out of a lot of money before.

Bobcat smiled at the frown on Red's face. "The Eight-Ball in the side pocket," chortled Bobcat. He was all smiles.

"Fifty more dollars says you can't make that shot without scratching!" said Big-Red, trying to ice Bobcat.

"You're on, Red," Bobcat chortled again. He was so confident.

Bobcat sighted the Eight-Ball over and over again. He walked back and forth around the table to look at how to shoot that shot from every angle. He cleared his throat, and beads of sweat formed on his forehead and nose. He slowly stroked his pool stick, readying to tap the cue easy and low. "This is for the money, Red," he said, and got ready to stroke her home.

Ty and his boy tipped up on Bobcat and Ty bumped him. The pool stick tapped the cue and it went askew.

"Now, you got to s'cuse me, home-slice!" said Ty, holding out his hands like he was really sorry. His walk-partner backed up towards an adjacent wall. He had his hand in his pocket on his gun.

Big-Red ran off the low-balls in a hurry, and sank the Eight-Ball for the game. "Sorry, my-man. Those are the breaks," he said. "Pay up!"

Ty clapped his hands when Big-Red sank the winning shot, and got paid.

Bobcat turned and hit Ty a popping lick to the jaw. It knocked him back but not down or out.

Ty pulled out his gun. The place emptied except for Gabe and Ty's walk-partner, who also had a gun drawn.

Ty fired once. It didn't stop Bobcat. He fired again and again, till his gun was empty. Bobcat's blood splattered all over the walls of the pool hall, on the doors and the floor, too. He reached Ty, with his left hand outstretched, and touched Ty with the tips of his fingers, then fell to the floor with a "thud!" A blood puddle trailed off from Bobcat, making a little stream, as his life flowed away out of him.

Gabe ran out of the place in shock. Ty stood poised with the gun, pulling the trigger a seventh and eighth time. His glassy eyes took on a sinister gaze like a demon from hell. He dropped the gun and knelt to the floor. "I ain't never killed nobody before ... I should've never killed nobody! ... What the hell am I go do, now! ..." chanted Ty. The stench of death filled up Taylor's. Old Jake kept his eye on Ty while calling the police. Worm was long gone.

"Y'all come on up here! Got another shooting!" said Jake. He hung the phone up, and spoke aloud. "Why y'all got to end the beefs you start with one-another down here in my place? Look at this crap! I've got to clean up this mess. You silly fools are killing one-another off like some disease. Over what? Over some stupid crap–I'll tell you what! When will y'all learn, you ignorant sons of Baal are doing the white man a favor. All he got to do is sat back and watch y'all kill one-another off one or two at a time–look at you!" yelled Jake at Ty.

Officers Gillen and Pace, along with Detective Doll, rushed over to Jake Taylor's. They took one look at Bobcat and smiled. "The coroner will take care of him," said Doll. He didn't even bother to examine the body or to check to see if Bobcat was still alive. He grabbed Ty up and ordered him, "Come with us Tyrone, boy. We got to do some talking," said Doll.

Gabe had made it around the corner to the foot of the Hill. He heard conversations that put more fear in him than anything else he had heard or seen while living on Vinegar Hill. He heard Doll say to Ty:

"You done us a darn good service, Ty. But we got to book you! Got to go through the routine–you know? You just got to lay low. Plead guilty. Let the law take its course. You won't do but a little time. Things got to look good," said Doll.

"Just keep your mouth shut," said Gillen. "Don't even talk to no reporters. Let us handle all of the publicity. You're our *Ace-Boon-Coon!*"

"You heard them," said Pace.

"Yessir! Yessir! Yessir!" went Ty.

"Let me remove those cuffs. I know you're hungry. The kitchen's closed over at the Jail, but I'll run out to a restaurant and find you something to eat. Mr. DiCappio left some money for you. Boy, you're our 'Nigger!' and we're going to lookout for you," said Doll. "We got a thousand dollars we going to hold till after this is over in the court and all. We got to make sure everything goes all right, first–you understand?"

"A thousand dollars?" exclaimed Ty. "He said I'd get five-thousand dollars for the job. I kept my part of the deal ..." whined Ty.

"Hold it right there, Ty! Boy, you ain't in no position to argue with us. I can keep every penny of the money and not give you a dime. Now, Mr. Dicappio and all of us wanted that Bobcat-buck dead. But we ain't obligated to you at all for killing him–is that clear?" shouted Doll. "From where I stand, a thousand dollars seem like a fortune for you–you got that?"

They dragged Ty up after they finished talking to him, threw him in a patty-wagon, and drove on off with him. Gabe trembled all over at what he had seen and heard. He ran out on Ridge Street, and just kept walking for a while to nowhere.

CHAPTER 24

▼

Tee just withdrew from the world after her son was murdered like he was. She remained silent for several days, not uttering a word. She wouldn't let George, Sr. touch her or come near her. Then on this Friday she called Gabe to her room. She was still in bed. "Come in Gabe," said Tee.

"How you doing, Mrs. Hinter?" asked Gabe.

"I'm still wondering where all of them people we don't know came from to Junior's funeral. Oakwood was filled up. Do you know who bought all them flowers? I didn't have no money, since I stopped pushing numbers for the mob. Big George didn't have any money to speak of either. Who do you reckon sent all those flowers?" said Mrs. Hinter. She cried like a little girl. Gabe caressed her gently.

"I reckon a lot of people liked George, Jr. He was kind to a lot of people on the Hill. He was a kind of 'Robin Hood,' I guess. That's why he got into trouble. White folk want the 'Robin Hood' fable to apply only to them. That's why everyone Bobcat helped came out to Zion Union. I bet, each one bought a wreath, or some floral arrangement," said Gabe, to Comfort Tee, as she leaned back onto her silk pillow. *Bobcat got what he deserves, but I'll comfort Mrs. Tee,* thought Gabe.

"Gabriel, I'm going to leave this town as soon as I can get myself together. I've never been happy down here. It's too far South. I'm going back to D.C.," said Mrs. Hinter. She pulled the covers tightly around her youthful looking figure. "I've given George all of my youth. Our only son is dead. That boy was like a 'Prince' to me. I was his 'Queen Mother.' I raised him that way. Maybe, I spoiled him, Gabe," said Mrs. Hinter.

"Don't even go there. It's not your fault, Mrs. Hinter. We all have choices. Sometimes we decide to do the wrong things. Then, life will turn on us. Some of the consequences are cruel and unforgiving. But there is an 'Afterlife' and we can hope to see our loved ones in the hereafter. So, take heart. Think of George, Jr., as one of the 'Guardians,'" said Gabe. "He's one of our 'Great Ancestors,' now."

"Gabriel. You are an 'Angel.' You're going to make some lucky girl a good husband one of these days. My man, he's an 'Ol' Uncle Tom.' He's a 'white-folks' Nigger!' I left Washington to come down here to marry George, years ago. I had a Nursing Degree from Howard University. When I got down here to Charlottesville, they wanted me to work as a Nurse's Aide. I got pregnant with Junior, before I could make up mind to leave George and this Godfor-saken-pit-of-racists down here. I always knew it would end badly for all of us. Gabe, my husband has a white woman that he's slipping around with. Been sneaking around with that little blond-hussy for almost a year, now! I know all about it. You can't do nothing in this little town without everybody getting the news right away. You see, I don't care. We haven't been happy with each other for years, now. Junior was all that we had in common. Now, he's gone, and I'll be gone next," Mrs. Hinter moaned out the words, almost bringing tears to Gabe's eyes.

"Is there any way that I can talk you out of it, Mrs. Tee?" asked Gabe.

"No, darling. I feel used up. This is not the way I wanted my life to be. When George was an Army Private stationed in Maryland, he was so much the man. I thought he was so handsome in his brown khaki-Uniform and spit-shined shoes. He swept me off my feet. But as the years went by, I became second-best to ... well ... to the whole white race. That's what George loves. That man would bend over backwards to please them, but look apathetically away when they are doing us in," said Tee.

Gabe found her statement puzzling. "What did he do? I mean, how did ..."

"Gabe, Tony DiCappio arranged to have Junior killed. George knows that. Junior wouldn't deal drugs for him. Wouldn't write numbers for him either. Up in D.C., heads would roll. The 'hood would be all over this thing. But my George, well ... he's just like the rest. Won't stand up! Let the man run all over him. Sometimes, I think they all act just like some old grinning, dancing Jim Crows! 'Yessir, mas'er! Yessir, mas'er!' that's what they're all about. They're marching in the streets, begging for what's rightfully theirs already. Honey, we just need to stand up to these racist jackals around here. A lot of things would change overnight," said Tee.

"Just like my daddy, they're afraid of what might happen to them, their families, and their manhood, if they dare do anything back, Mrs. Hinter," complained Gabe.

"Yeah. You're right. But the truth is, as long as we allow them to come over here and do what they want to us, whenever they get ready, and we do nothing about it, we will always be under their feet," said Tee. "Turn your back, son. Let me get up and put on my robe."

Gabe turned his back, but sneaked a peek. Tee got up and quickly put on her African robe with it's Kenti Cloth print. She sat down in a black fluffy love seat, and slipped on a pair of glossy-black, leather sandals. She crossed her beautiful legs.

"When Bill Griot was killed, I threatened Doll and them. I knew they liked picking on Junior and his friends. I told him that if he ever tried to do Junior in, I'd tell the FBI, NAACP, and whomever, what I know! I told him, that I would broadcast to the world that Clemmon Doll and his cousins are 'Negroes,' and furnish the evidence to prove it. They left me and Junior alone after that! ..."

So, that's where it's at. That's the leverage that Mrs. Hinter have over ol' Doll and them. That's why Bobcat never got arrested. The cops were afraid that their dirty little secret would get out. They were trying to erase all knowledge about who they are. That's why Mrs. Tee is leaving from around here. I'm going too. I know they're going to figure out that I know way too much. Even old George is in danger! thought Gabe.

Mrs. Hinter grew farther and farther away from old George. Ideologically, they were miles apart. Separation was inevitable. The day came for Mrs. Tee to just leave. George was out with his white woman. He was spending more and more time sneaking around with her. Gabe and everyone knew that. The day came when Gabe helped Mrs. Tee to the C&O Train Station. Her train was not long in coming; and, Gabe watched as the porters loaded all of Mrs. Orthilia Hinter's white Samsonite suitcases onto the train. The dainty, beautiful lady, kissed him on his cheek, and then quite surprised him. She kissed him on his lips, a long lingering kiss.

"I wish I could be the woman to bring out the best in you, Gabe, darling. But time and circumstances have gotten in our way. If you are ever up in the D.C. area, come over to Howard University's campus, you'll find me at their hospital. I'm going to be a Registered Nurse there. I see you as one of my best friends," said Mrs. Tee. Tears streamed down her cheeks as she boarded the train, and it slowly started down the tracks. She waved from a window, and Gabe waved back. He fought back the tears.

This is the second-best lady in my life. Momma is the first. I love them both for what they have meant to me. I know I'm going to see Mrs. Tee again some day. I hope she finds all the best wherever she lands, thought Gabe.

Gabe wept!

PART III

▼

CHAPTER 25

▼

"Mr. Hinter, I think it's time for me to move on. I appreciate all that you and Mrs. Hinter did to help me get started. I will never forget either of you; George, Jr., neither," said Gabe.

"Well ... I'm kind of glad you came to that decision. Son, I'm going to move off this Hill soon anyway. I've been seeing a lady I think I'm going to end up with. I know you've heard," uttered Mr. Hinter.

"I don't pay no attention to the 'grapevine' Mr. Hinter," said Gabe, smiling sheepishly.

"By the way, you can pack up all of those papers and things that you want out of that room. I'll probably throw whatever you leave behind away. I don't have no use for any of it. I ain't one to stir up nothing at all. Getting along, that's how I've survived all these years. I just couldn't get Junior to go along with me. You know, he'd be alive today if he had listened to me instead of ..." said Mr. Hinter, stopping short of accusing Tee.

"We all got to struggle in our own way. One might not all the time agree with the other. That's not unity, but we Blacks have that to rise up to. As long as we aren't sitting still, that's what will keep us down," said Gabe.

"Well, little Gabe. Here's my hand to you. Let's part friends. I wish you all the best. You are a smart young man. Put the key in the mail slot when you finish moving all your things out. If I don't see you again, have a good life, my-man," said old George, extending his hand to Gabe.

"Thank you, very much, Mr. Hinter," said Gabe, then he shook hands with old George, vigorously, for the last time.

Gabe got a room at Vera's house. It was more like a closet, big enough for a fold-up cot, with shelves around the top of it. He felt like it was all that he needed for the meantime. He eventually moved all of Bill Griot's books and papers into the little closet, making the place seem like the abode of a packrat. When Mary Lou and Brenda went out–which they did daily–Gabe would scribble some notes he had been compiling about what he had learned about Vinegar Hill. He had over twenty-pages, so far. Besides, now and then, he got a chance to hook up with Brenda, too.

On this morning, Gabe was awakened by loud talking.

"What's that in the mail momma?" asked Mary Lou. The postman had left an official-looking letter in the mailbox. A little chilly wind twirled the leaves all around the Hill that seemed to come from the direction of McGuffrey Hill. The sun barely broke through the layered clouds, casting a hazy light over Charlottes-ville.

"I don't know what's in no letter, child. We ain't 'specting no 'ficial letter from nobody," yelled Vera, looking tired as hell from scrubbing City Hall's floors, and like she wished her daughters would be more considerate of her and not bother her for every little detail.

"Y'all go on out there. Get the darn mail. See what's in the doggone letter. I needs my sleep y'all, okay?" complained Vera. "Wish y'all would quiet down so I can even go back to sleep. They busy down at that Midway Building these days."

Mary Lou darted outside to get the letter. She came right back into the door sweating like it was hot outside, like in July.

"Wait momma, it's from the City Council," said Mary Lou with her smooth ebony-hands trembling from her deeply-felt fears.

Vera came running out of her room wearing a long, cotton, robe, with red, green and black stripes all over it, like the Afro-American flag. "What's in that let-ter, y'all," she blurted out. "Some say the city's go rebuild these old places 'round here, and bring'em up to standards. I hope they ain't go tear this building down. It's our home. I don't want to go nowheres else in this city to live–that's what I feels way down in my heart," whined little, old, Vera Crenshaw.

Mary Lou tore the brown manilla envelope open. She pulled out a one-page letter bearing the city's logo.

"Go ahead on, read that darn letter, Mary Lou. Well–what do it say?" shot out of Vera's tired trembling lips. She meant to scratch her head, but undid one the small bobby-pins in her hair. It fell to the floor.

Mary Lou looked down at the letter. "Well momma, it says: 'Dear Vera, et al., We regret to have to inform you that as of the end of October, 1963, you and all occupants on the premises at 1301 Third Street, will have to yield up the property; for it is no longer owned by Mr. Brice Lamb; but has been acquired, by right of Eminent Domain, by The Charlottesville Housing Development Cooperative.

"'If you have any questions concerning the contents of this letter, or if you have difficulties finding suitable living quarters, call us at the numbers listed below. We will assist you in any way that we can. Signed: Mayor, Horace Bowles, and City Manager, Cooley Mason.'"

Mary Lou finished reading the hateful message, folded up the letter, then her hands trembled all over, like she had the chills. Brenda joined her sister in trembling. Both of the young women started to cry softly. They ran over to Vera.

"Momma, Councilman Lamb done sold this house right from under us! I guess we got to go on our merry little way, or something," screamed Brenda.

"We done been paying our rent on time for years, now. Ain't never been behind. That ought to count for something. I guess we's like fleas on a dog's back! They're shoving us off this hill! They ain't go rebuild nothing at all!" shouted Mary Lou.

May Lou opened her eyes. She missed her momma. Then she spied Vera. Gabe was kneeling down beside her. She was laid out on the floor, with her eyes closed, her raisin-like face was balling up tight. Her full lips opened as she gasped for breath. Her right hand clutched under her left breast. Her left hand clawed the floor. She got splinters in that hand. The fingernails of it got ripped off. They bled. Vera's eyes opened, then rolled back up into her head. Her labored breaths ceased after gushing out of her mouth for the last time, gone like the wind of October in November. The chill of death engulfed the room, the house, and the neighborhood.

"Momma! ... Momma! ... Don't go! ..." screamed Mary Lou.

"God! ... God! ... Help us! ..." screamed Brenda.

Gabe ran out to call Yellow Cab to come transport Vera's lifeless body to the hospital, so that a coroner could pronounce the obvious. And, so it happened.

Two days after the death of Vera, Gabe got a room at Jake Taylor's boarding house over on Lankford Avenue. He was there on this morning, when an official-looking letter came to Jake and them.

"Jake–Jake, boy, what you got out there in the mailbox?" said an old scratcher, wearing Bibb overalls, shiny-black old folk's comforts, and a red flannel shirt. His big old beer-gut bounced when he talked. He was Duke Taylor, Jake's father.

"Daddy, I think it's another one of them darn proposals again," said Jake. He had on his daily black trousers, white shirt, and a little black bow tie. He seemed to always dress the same way everyday.

Duke scratched his fluffy graying salt-and-pepper hair, and then his link-sausage nose, took the letter from his son's hand, rubbed his graying mustache, and cleared his throat.

"Look out now, we ain't gonna do nothing in a rush," said Duke. A note of cautious fear ringing in his voice. "They's out to get Black folks out of they property, and that's for doggone sure," he shot out of his time-wrinkled lips. "Jake, get me my reading glasses off the cupboard. Let me see what those jackals downtown done cooked up this time."

Old Duke read the letter he had pulled out of a big manilla envelope very quickly. "We won't do it ... I tell you, they's trying to steal our businesses right from under our noses. We done worked for them businesses all of our lives. Jake, your mother Judy died working right beside me to help build something to leave you and my future grandchildren. I ain't got much ed-di-cation, I know. But I can read well enough to see through this crap on this letter," yelled old Duke. "You got a good ed-di-cation, Jake. You got to fight for the future I'm trying to build for you."

"Don't worry daddy. I'll get back everything they think they're going to take from us. You didn't work in vain. I'm a handle it right," said Jake. Both men struggled with powerful, gripping, emotions.

"Daddy, let's call Chuck in the morning. I know he's in court till late today. If it's all right with you, I'd just as soon wait till in the morning to call Chuck's office, okay?" said Jake. "Sometimes, I wish some of them militants would fire-bomb that bunch down at the Midway Building!"

On the next day: "Hello, there. Is this Chuck Brown's office?" asked Jake. His voice shaking more with each word he uttered.

"Yes, this is Mr. Chuck Brown's office, Attorney at Law. How may we help you, sir?" a sing-song white-female's voice answered.

"Hi, Clara, I'm Jake Taylor. I need to speak with Mr. Brown. He's representing me and daddy on a case."

"Oh, yes, I recognize your voice, now. I'll see if Mr. Brown is in," chimed Clara.

"Hey, buddy. This is me, old Chuck. What is happening, now?" he asked, in his characteristically baritone voice, sounding like a modified Perry Mason.

"We got another crappy offer from the City Council yesterday. We're getting plucked like a goose. They're offering chicken feed," whined Jake.

"I know, Jake. These crooks downtown are just out to move you people off that Hill is all. It's a darn shame, too. Y'all made them who they are and that's for darn sure," said Chuck.

"Can you just get them to up the ante to a reasonable settlement, Chuck?" asked Jake, plaintively.

"I'll go over there to the City Council and shake them good old boys up. I'll get you a … very good settlement, I assure you, Jake," said Chuck.

"Thank you, Chuck. I knew we could count on you. We always have," said Jake with cautious optimism.

The phone rang in the Taylor's living room, and Jake ran to it. Gabe was sitting in one of their fine black leather front room sofas. They had two and two end chairs to match. Their green, plush carpet was kept dazzling clean by Sadie, Jake's shapely, beautiful, very light-skinned wife. She more resembled a sandy-haired, gray-eyed, five-foot, white woman. She had a brilliant smile. She walked about slowly and gracefully, like royalty. Her hair was naturally wavy, and she just parted it in the middle of her head and let it flow down to her waist. Gabe wondered: *Is Sadie an unlikely one, passing for Black?* Sadie stood beside her husband as he answered the phone.

"Well, hello, Jake. It's old Chuck, here. We got a better deal with those scoundrels over at Midway," said Chuck, exuberantly.

"Good. How much did you get them up to?" asked Jake.

"I got them up to fifty-thousand. I had to put a mighty twist on their arms to get them up to that. I know, your property is worth more than they are offering, but they aren't going to budge...."

"What you say, Chuck? They just going to raise up the offer from Thirty-nine to fifty thousand. That's still chicken feed. The inventory in our Grocery Store is worth more than that; not to mention the equipment in our Barbershop; and in our Restaurant. We're being swindled. We will never be able to replace all we're losing with fifty-thousand, nowadays!" yelled Jake into the phone.

Duke snatched the phone out of Jake's hand.

"Have you forgotten who I am, Chuck. I've spent thousands of dollars with you in the past. You know we ought not to get less than seventy-five thousand dollars for that property over on the Hill. It's not rundown. It's not ruined. I've kept it up all these years. What are we s'pose to do?" yelled Duke.

Duke dropped the phone and crumbled to the floor. His eyes closed, his body trembled, and he gave up the ghost. The shock brought on a massive heart attack.

Sadie grabbed Jake and clutched her frightened husband to her bosom. She tried to console Jake. She could not. His complexion turned orange, then greenish-gray. His eyes narrowed like a cat's at night. His lips trembled like a little child that had forgotten how to speak. His hands shook a little at first, then violently. He backed away from Sadie. She and Gabe watched Jake take leave of his right mind. The foam forming at the corners of his mouth confirmed his mental state. He had lost it.

"What am I going to do now? My father-in-law is dead! And, my husband's mind is gone!" screamed Sadie.

"Mrs. Taylor, if there is anything I can do to help you, just tell me what," said Gabe. Tears came to his young eyes that he couldn't keep from escaping down his cheeks.

"Yes, Gabe. Yes indeed," said Sadie with a sarcastic sigh.

Gabe watched her arrange for old Duke's funeral, put her husband in Central State Mental Health facility, and she somehow found the strength to run the boarding house. It was all she had left.

Chuck Brown sent her a check for the settlement with the City Council for Forty-thousand dollars minus his fee of ten-thousand-dollars; and, that was that.

CHAPTER 26

▼

Gabe rented a room with Mrs. Sadie Taylor through the Winter of 1963, and the Spring of 1964. He took walks downtown during this time to see what was happening.

Each day that Gabe visited Vinegar Hill he saw more buildings becoming empty, vacant, dead. *I wish I had had nothing to do with this crap at all. Maybe, if I hadn't called the cops and squealed on Bobcat and them, this wouldn't have happened. I feel like I helped the "Pigs" kill Vinegar Hill. I just wanted to do what was right! Dog, man! Now, I feel like I helped them murder an entire Black neighborhood. What am I going to do, now?* thought Gabe.

Gabe sobbed some days: *It is so gut-wrenching for me to see all these buildings on Vinegar Hill vacant and silent, and I see the blight of Random Row devouring the whole of the Hill like a cancer that overtakes the human body.*

The chant of little children can no longer be heard in the streets anymore. Young men and women will no longer hold hands in courtship anymore. The little old ladies will not stand watch over their beloved community each morning. The old-timers with their faded Jeans, and their fables will never stand In The Streets of Vinegar Hill and regale youngsters with tales of their youthful exploits anymore. Gone! Gone! Gone! It's all Gone! Gabe lamented.

In March, 1964 the bulldozers owned by Morrison, Bowles and DiCappio came and started their hateful work. They reached in and ripped out a hunk of the downtown area that had stood there for over a hundred years. They flushed the poor people out of their places like a dog does a rabbit from its hiding. There was nothing left but a huge gaping hole, and despair, anger, and Black-frustration, as insult was added to injury. The same construction firms: Bowles, Morrison and DiCappio got the contracts to build a quickly erected "Project" on Hardy Drive called "Wesley's Haven." It was pasted together rather loosely with pipes exposed in the ceilings of the houses that were jammed together like cracker-boxes. This was where Mary Lou and Brenda ended up with two children each and about a hundred or so other people. The place was a slum from the start. It was worse than Vinegar Hill from the beginning. (It was four blocks closer to the campus of the UVA.)

Gabe heard what happened to Doll through the "Grapevine."

"Doll, come over to my office, you and Officers, Gillen and Pace. We got to go over some important matters. This is what the Council wants me to tell y'all," said Mayor Bowles. "It's some of my last official acts before I go out of office."

"Okay, Mr. Bowles," said Doll. He called Pace and Gillen on his CB and had them meet with him and the Mayor over at Midway.

After they had all arrived, Mayor Bowles said, "Y'all come on into the Council's Chambers where we won't be disturbed."

They all entered the Chambers and Mayor bowles fastened the doors. "Sit down, gentlemen. I got a little bar set up in here, today. Y'all go on get yourselves a little drink of that J&B Scotch. It's the best stuff I ever drunk," said Mayor Bowles.

"No, I'm on duty," said Doll.

"No! ... I'm the boss. Y'all have my permission to drink up. I insist," said Mayor Bowles.

The cops got water glasses, filled them with ice, and poured liquor over the crushed ice. All four of the men sipped out of their drinks.

Mayor Bowles' eyes got sad as he began to speak: "I'm so proud of the job y'all have been doing for the city. Let me tell you, I can't put my finger on any other cops on the force I'm more proud of than y'all three," he said. Then he gulped down his scotch, and poured himself another glassful. "Drink up, gentlemen," he said.

"That Chuck Brown–a fraggin' 'Nigger-Lover!'–filed a report with the NAACP, and the Federal Civil Rights Commission. The Justice Department is going to come down on us real hard, men," said Bowles. "We all got to cover our butts."

"What does that mean, Horace?" asked Doll.

"The Council feels that I have to ask you boys to resign for the good of Charlottesville. We're going to have to hire three bucks to replace y'all. That is the only way we will be able to make this do-do go away. Hell, I hate to be the one to tell y'all this. But, I got this crap dumped in my lap. We will give y'all the best recommendations possible. Y'all...."

"Oh, shut the hell up, Horace. I don't want to hear another doggone word. Up-you and the Council!" replied Gillen. He slammed his badge and gun on the table and marched out of the place.

"That's how I see it too, Horace!" said Pace. He also turned in his badge and gun before leaving.

"Now, it's just you and me, Horace. I know too doggone much for you to just shed me like a snake does his skin. I can actually put your butt in prison," Doll shouted at Horace.

"No ... You just wait a minute! Let me put all of this in perspective. Arthur Gilbert is a liberal. Don't know how that Democrat fell through the cracks. He found out about everything. He's in with Chuck Brown, Reverend Bower, and that NAACP crowd, Clemm. We don't have a chance ..." said Horace, with a little grimace.

"If we all stick to our guns, we'd have more than a chance. The people around here ain't going to side with Chuck Brown and them. You can dig up the dirt on Arthur. I know there's got to be some," said Clemm.

"No there isn't, Clemm; and Chuck has already cost us eleven grand!"

"How in the hell did Gilbert even get elected, then, Horace?"

"Clemm. This is a new day. Those Civil Rights Bills are going to pass. They killed that Kennedy boy, and now the sympathy in this Country is with his family and in what JFK stood for. The Bills are going to pass. Johnson is one of the greatest, dirt-busting, politicians ever to grace the White House. He's behind those Civil Rights Bills, now Clemm, and they're going to become law; trust me!"

"I won't go quietly, Horace. Y'all owe me!"

Horace turned and stepped to Clemm. He pointed his trigger finger right into Clemm's face. His lips peeled back so that his teeth looked like an Opossum's.

"Now! You little high-yellow, 'Nigger!' You shut your doggone mouth. Yeah, we all know that you are not white! I've known for the longest time. We did a background check on your family's history sometime ago. We found out that you are a little half-white bastard. Guess what! I can have you arrested right now. You're illegally living with a white woman. You're illegally holding a job in the police department. That's a position for a white man," Horace belted out.

Tears came to the corners of Clemm's eyes as he got hit with the terrible truth.

"So, Clemm, you'll get the hell out of this building, after you leave that gun and your badge behind, and I wouldn't recommend you for the job of dog-catcher," screamed Horace.

Clemm drew his police revolver. "Don't move, Horace. Right now, I don't have much to lose. I just as soon shoot as not!" said Clemm as he backed away from Horace. His heartbeat thumped like a drum; his head throbbed with every beat; and his blood rushed to his head. He could taste it in his mouth.

"Let me warn you. Get your black ass out of town, 'Nigger!' Do that as soon as possible. Then I'll not tell the world out there that your darling little girls are not white. They can pass and go on off to college and marry some nice white guys. No one will be the wiser," said Horace with a smirk on his fat face.

Clemm took out his badge and threw it at Horace. He turned and ran out of the Chambers.

Horace ran back to his office, got on a CB and issued an All-Points-Bulletin:

"All cars be on alert. Ex-Detective Clemm Doll has illegally commandeered a police vehicle. He has refused to turn in his police special sidearm. He's highly agitated, and is considered armed and dangerous. Please apprehend him with extreme caution...."

Doll arrived home that evening, jumped out of his police cruiser, and dashed into his home. "Got to get in before Brenda comes to work. Got to ..." he whined.

Once in the front room, he called out: "Polly, I got to get you and the kids away from here. We got to go North, honey!" he yelled, frantically. "Polly, where are you? You should be home! ..."

Doll ran from room to room, no Polly, nor Carol, or Charlotte. "Polly, where can you be?" screamed Doll, as all of his grip on rationality started to ebb away. "You better not be fooling around with me!"

Then he saw a folded up letter lying on the bed in the master bedroom. He ran over and scooped it up. He read it aloud:

"Dear Clemmon, I and the girls have gotten tired of your beatings and harassment. We are tired of your hatred for your own people. I've always known, even before we got pregnant with Carol, that you were 'Colored.' It never mattered to me. The girls know too. I told them. They didn't mind—nobody else knew, or didn't care. We just kept it to ourselves, so the neighbors wouldn't talk and all. But, you just kept on and on. I'm too tired of that, Clemm. I don't love you anymore, and your daughters hate you, too. We all want out of the mess you've made of yourself and our lives.

"Let me be the first to tell you, that I have met another nice 'Colored' man. He promises that he will help undo the damage you have inflicted on all of us. He's just as sweet as you are mean. I like him very much and will come to love him. The girls think the world of him. He'll be a much better father figure than you ever were. He, the girls and I are heading North. You will not be able to find us, so don't try.

"I hope you will stop hating yourself. All hatred is intuitive. The hate you project onto light-skinned 'Negroes,' is really how you hate yourself, that's all, Clemm. Please stop this. It's so self-destructive.

"Forgive me for all of the pain this letter is going to cause you. I never wanted to hurt you. I'm just sorry that you could never work out in your own mind the problem of your having 'Colored-Blood' in your veins. We all do, you know. I hope your girls will one day come to forgive you, too. Right now, they want nothing at all to do with you; nor do I. Signed: Polly Doll."

"Oh, God. What am I going to do, now! I can't undo the damage," screamed Doll. He didn't hear Brenda come into the house. The front door had been left open. She saw Doll put the nozzle of his police special against his forehead. Brenda was petrified with fear. She slipped just around the corner. She heard Doll confessing:

"Oh, God, before I come up there, I got to confess. Me and Pace stalked William Griot. We caught him, took him over to Random Row, and beat him to death with a rubber hose. I'm sorry, Lord. Forgive me.

"Me and Gillen caught up with James Killeen over near the C&O station. We beat him with axe handles until Pace came along and shot him. I'm sorry Lord.

"We all took part in killing and hanging Leroy Quayles up yonder on the old Oak tree. Forgive me, Lord ..."

The hand that Doll held the gun in trembled like he was having a spasm. He slowly took the gun from his forehead, put the barrel into his mouth, and pulled the trigger. Brenda screamed as she witnessed Doll's brains and blood spewing out of his head up to the ceiling, on the rug on the floor and splattering on the wall. Doll slumped over to the floor convulsing for a few seconds, then a stream of blood trailed off from the head of his still, lifeless, body.

Vomit came up Brenda's throat as she ran out of the house screaming. Police cars came around the street corners with their sirens blasting. They were sent to arrest Doll. All they got to do was collect his corpse.

A rookie cop came into Chief Moon's office out of breath and highly excited.

"Sir, Detective Doll blew his own brains out," he said.

"Ain't that just like a 'Nigger!'"said Moon, nonchalantly.

After all of the experiences I've had, and all of the stories I've heard, I understand what the ghost of Bill Griot was trying to tell me. He was trying to get me to under-stand that racial-fears are a kind of "Goliath." It is all pervasive, violence-prone, emo-tionally crippling, and morally paralyzing. This "Giant," like the Biblical one, is responsible for the lion's share of social, political and economical problems in Charlot-

tesville, America and the world. Everyone has to defeat their own version of "Goliath" before he can truly be free. Otherwise, he will always be just a slave to his own inner-fear: "The Fear Of The Unknown."

Thought Gabe.

EPILOGUE

▼

Gabe stood on the edge of what was once Vinegar Hill in the downtown area of Charlottesville, Virginia. It was late afternoon. The sun felt warm against his back. The August dog-days were letting up a little as the last days of August neared. It was 1996. He had turned forty-nine that year. He had been away from Charlottesville for thirty-two years.

In 1964, Gabe had gone to Washington, D.C., to Howard University. He first studied for a while at Morgan State College's Remedial Training Center and earned his GED certificate. He then went on to Howard to earn his BS., ME., and Ph.D., degrees in Social Studies. He taught school at Dunbar High School.

On this day, Gabe came back to Charlottesville to reminisce, and to recapture the feelings he had almost totally forgotten. He stood on the edge of the Hill and could see that the area had been rebuilt. Over the years, the gaping hole had been filled in. His heart beat out the rhythms of anguish again like a Jazz drummer.

Gabe looked around a little and noticed that where Third Street used to be, a grand hotel stood. It was on the order of a Hilton, Ramada Inn, or DoubleTree hotel. He remembered that DiCappio, a mafia boss, owned a large hotel chain. Over across the street from it, was a huge skating rank. Ex-Mayor Bowles, a construction mogul, his company had built that building as well as the hotel. Ex-Councilman Morrison was dead but his family, along with the family of Ex-Councilman Lamb still were the largest building contractors in Charlottesville. They were contracted to build a Virginia Employment Commission building. They built an IGA grocery store right next to it; a federal building next to that; and up from there, on Random Row, they had built a strip-mall. Every kind of business and greasy-spoon restaurant stood over there.

Zion Union had been torn down. Gabe heard that it had been reestablished up on the other end of Preston Avenue. Where it once stood was now a huge parking lot for the Jefferson Middle School and Carver Recreational Center. The little store on the corner of Fourth and West Main had become a Bar. There were no Black-owned businesses left on the Hill. That realization brought tears to Gabe's eyes. *What a shame!* thought Gabe. *The whole twenty-acre tract has no Blacks left on it!*

Everything on the Hill is white-owned now. My people are displaced. They are in the "Projects" on Prospect Avenue, Hardy Drive, Mountainwood Road, Garret Square, and Lankford and Cherry Avenues. These are all drug-dealing, crime-infested slums. Everywhere Black people exist in Charlottesville in government-sponsored "Projects," drug-trafficking prevails. This infestation is very prevalent wherever poor Blacks are clustered. Like at Garret Square–on Garret Street–First Street, Southwest; Tenth and Page Streets; and at Washington Park, on the Northwest side of town. Drugs and their accompanying violence ensue and local law enforcement all but ignores these areas, just like it had Vinegar Hill.

The thoughts of his mind, and the meditations of his heart made Gabe feel sick to his stomach, when he came to grips with the knowledge that young Blacks were killing each other very violently and often, just like in D.C., Jersey, and New York.

I know. I'll come back to this area next fall. I'll find a way to convince my wife, Audrey, and Gabe, Jr., both professionals, to come back here with me. We can make a difference. Just like I forgave daddy for taking his fears out on me, using "That Old Segregation Crap!" as an excuse to project his angst onto me, that he felt against the system, that had caused him all of his pains, I have forgiven these people. We are all victims of the same system. When dad was lowered into the ground, it hurt me to my heart. He'd been dead for so long before then. He was dead to real love; dead to any hope for a better future; dead to any recognition of his historical "Self," and what his African Heritage meant to him and all of our descendants from Africa. When they threw the dirt on his casket in 1983, I let go of any hate, and or resentment, I had kept locked up in me over the years for my father. All of that got buried with him; and I whispered, "Rest In Peace, Daddy! Momma's love still keeps us all alive. She will live in us forever!" Even though she had gone to be with the "Ancestors" in 1980.

My wife Audrey is the product of a white man's rape upon her mother who had been a maid in this so-called "upstanding white-citizen's" home in Alexandria, Virginia. She's been through a lot and has a lot of sophisticated things to say and teach to downtrodden, Black Charlottesvillians. My son is a lawyer trained at Howard in its best tradition. He knows just how to handle the racial and racist situations still very prevalent in Charlottesville.

I'll go up to Maryland and get them and bring them back here with me. "Yes, I'll be back!" crowed Gabe, pumping his right fist into the air with great force.

The sun slowly slid behind the horizon. A cool breeze crept down the streets. Seemed like a cold hand patted Gabe on his back. The pants legs of his charcoal-gray, two-piece, suit began to shimmy. As Gabe walked away from the edge of the Hill, he yelled into the night, "I'll be back next year!" With his left hand, he pressed his red-green-and-black striped tie against his light-green, silk shirt, held up his head and strolled on into the rest of his life. *Think I ought to write a book about all this,* thought Gabe....

(Chuck [Charles] Brown and Arthur B. Gilbert were law-partners at the time that they swindled Duke, Jake and Sadie Taylor out of ten thousand dollars. They used the city's fear of the NAACP, and threatened that they would go to the Federal Justice Department, if the city did not pay them eleven thousand dollars. Only one of those thousands was added to the fanciful amount the city paid Sadie Taylor. Out of guilt, both Chuck and Arthur became Civil Rights lawyers and worked tirelessly, in conjunction with the NAACP, to implement the 1960s Black Civil Rights Legislation in Charlottesville. Today, they and also their sons, carry on the fight via the ACLU.)

978-0-595-42550-1
0-595-42550-X

Made in the USA
San Bernardino, CA
03 August 2016